Frederick William Faber, Auguste Gratry

The Month of Mary

Conceived without Sin

Frederick William Faber, Auguste Gratry

The Month of Mary
Conceived without Sin

ISBN/EAN: 9783742862778

Manufactured in Europe, USA, Canada, Australia, Japa

Cover: Foto ©Andreas Hilbeck / pixelio.de

Manufactured and distributed by brebook publishing software
(www.brebook.com)

Frederick William Faber, Auguste Gratry

The Month of Mary

THE MONTH OF MARY

CONCEIVED WITHOUT SIN.

TRANSLATED FROM THE FRENCH OF

A. GRATRY,

PRIEST OF THE ORATORY OF THE IMMACULATE CONCEPTION.

WITH AN INTRODUCTION

BY THE

VERY REV. F. W. FABER, D. D.,

OF THE LONDON ORATORY.

LONDON:
THOMAS RICHARDSON AND SON,
26, PATERNOSTER ROW ;
9, CAPEL STREET, DUBLIN; AND DERBY.

CONTENTS.

CONTENTS.

INTRODUCTION.

Every age of the Church is, in a certain
sense, more glorious than any of the ages
which have preceded it. It is true that there
have been special ages in which God has
magnified the Church more visibly than in
others, and has been pleased to illustrate it
with peculiar splendour: and these special
ages have by no means followed each other
in chronological succession. But on the whole
the glory of the Church increases with its age.
It becomes more famous by its very vicissitudes. Every trial through which it passes
is a fresh illumination of its divine origin and
its unearthly character. It grows more hon-
ourable by the mere force of time, because of
the increased number of dangers which it has
surmounted, of hostile predictions which it has
belied, and of grand human institutions which
it has outlived. Moreover the number of the
Saints in the Church Triumphant multiplies
yearly, and cannot be, according to St. Paul's
law of sympathy, without influence on the

Church Militant. Thus the past, as it departs, is for ever adorning the Church with beautiful monuments and interesting memorials, while the present, as it reinforces the multitudes of heaven, is for ever infusing fresh vigour, joy, and liberty into the Body upon earth.

But the additional splendour of the Church, with which we are most concerned at present, is the growth of its devotions. Although devotion comes out of doctrine, new devotions by no means imply new doctrines. Divine works are very vast and very fertile; and, if the least mystery of the Incarnation is probably unfathomable even by angelic intelligence, it cannot be a matter of surprise to us that the human mind, employed upon any of these mysteries in love and prayer, and often with infused wisdom from above, should be making continual discoveries of beauty, of pathos, or of significance. The riches of Christ in the Incarnation are simply unsearchable. They are thus able inexhaustibly to disclose themselves in new aspects and in new connections to the pure and sanctified mind. Furthermore, the characteristics of the mind of one century often differ materially from the genius of the mind of another century. The mind of any one age sees things from its own point of view, and reasons upon them in a way of its own ; and this of itself materially affects that body of devotional science which ages of meditation have brought together. Besides this, God is continually making private revelations to the Saints and Contemplatives; and these, in different degrees, are received into the mind of the Church, and predominate in popular devotion. Each Saint, as the Church tells us in the Divine Office, stands on an eminence of his own, which, though not necessarily higher than the eminences of other saints, is different from theirs, and is peculiarly his own. Thus each Saint for the most part leaves some impression of himself on the Church, and that impression is most likely to be traceable in popular devotion. Hence, while it is the property of beautiful things to expand and grow, it is the prerogative of the Church to be the place, the soil, and the climate in which this expansion shall be most luxuriant and graceful.

There is something very astonishing, while it is also very grateful to the pious mind, in the growth of devotion to our Blessed Lady in the Church. It is wonderful to see practices of devotion, which have now taken possession of the Catholic mind and become apparently inseparable from it; and yet to be able to

point to the individual Saint, or to the particular religious Order, out of whose character
and sanctity the practice came, and to quote
the date at which it first appeared in the
Church. Of a truth the life of the Church is
a very broadening thing, more so by far than
the life of the world. But in nothing has
this breadth been more palpable than in the
matter of devotions, and in no devotion more
signal than in that to our Blessed Lady. The
faithful know more of our Lady than they did
before. They know more of her, because they
are continually receiving fresh kindnesses from
her. The proofs of her power multiply. Her
miracles, her interventions, her apparitions,
her revelations, her pilgrimages—each century
adds to the amount of each one of these things,
and so to the proof of all of them. Thus
inevitable experience is always teaching the
faithful more about Mary, while meditation is
also adding to the bulk of our knowledge about
her. Just as increase of devotion to our
Blessed Lady is in the individual soul the
most unerring sign of growth in holiness, so is
it in the Church an infallible sign of the
broadening and deepening of its supernatural
life. The immense increase of devotion to
our Blessed Lady through the Definition of
the Immaculate Conception is the grandeur

and the jubilee of the present age of the Church.

It may also be remarked that times of unusual trouble for the Church have also been times of unusual developement of devotion to our Blessed Lady. This has partly arisen from the supernatural instinct which is always resident in the Church, and which is the law, sometimes consciously, sometimes unconsciously, of its life. Partly also it has come from the quickening of our faith in our Lady's greatness and queenship, which is itself the effect and the reward of our more vehement and urgent recourse to her protection. Besides this, the interests of the Church are in an especial manner her interests; and, as queen of the apostles, she watches with a particular vigilance over the fortunes of the Holy See. Hence it is that in almost all the great sorrows of the Holy See she has come forth, and revealed herself, in some striking manifestation. Nearly all the monuments of Church history are dedicated to Mary; and they are dedicated to her, not so much by the intelligent gratitude of the faithful, as by the very force of the events themselves. When we are removed to a sufficient distance from events to see them in their true proportions, in the aspect in which all truthful history will henceforth see them, then there is no avoiding the conviction that Mary is the star of the bark of Peter, and a star whose rays shine through the thickest night and the most terrific storms.

To all the faithful, therefore, devotion to our Blessed Mother is of supreme importance. It is not a mere beauty of catholic worship, a graceful accessory, an exquisite adornment, or a lawful consolation. It is an essential element in all Christian piety. Without it, holiness is simply impossible. But to us in an uncatholic country devotion to Mary assumes a very peculiar importance. We are surrounded on all sides by monuments of falsehood. The air is impregnated with its poison. The daily intercourse of life becomes almost a contagion of evil. Measures, weights, and standards, which are quite opposed to those of the sanctuary of God, are implied and acknowledged in the common language which we use, so that it is difficult to avoid making a material profession of an unholy faith even when we have no such intention. The literature of our country is perpetually imbuing us with unchristian principles, the more insidiously the more the subject of it is apparently removed from religion altogether. The habitual perusal of the protestant newspapers is itself as nearly as possible incompatible with the existence of the spirit of prayer, or with the preservation of intelligent catholic sympathies. The very sweetest and kindliest parts of our nature are perpetually alluring us to an easy and indulgent view of that deadliest of all sins, the sin of heresy, and thus to an acquiescence in that which ought both morally and intellectually to be the most repulsive of all things to us, falsehood about God.

Now devotion to Mary has been in all ages, as an historical fact, the guardian of the doctrine about Jesus. There need be no surprise to us in this. Certainly a theologian would have expected it beforehand, even if he had no acquaintance whatever with the history of doctrine. But what we are concerned with now is the practical lesson which this fact reads to ourselves. Devotion to our Blessed Lady must be our refuge from the presence and the oppression of the triumphant heresy round about us. Of all our gifts that of faith should be the dearest to us ; for it is the gift in which the secret of our strength consists, in which the sanctuary of our soul's life is placed. But growth in devotion to Mary is at the same time a growth in faith. By the pious observance of her feasts, by frequent meditation on her grandeurs, by an intelligent study of the theology which concerns her, by enrolment in her Confraternities, by habitual telling of her Beads, and by wearing her Scapulars, we are perpetually fortifying our faith, augmenting its quantity, and quickening its intensity. The vigour of our faith enables us to resist the infection of heresy, and to pass unscathed by the poison of its touch. We shall do wisely therefore, in the foul air of a protestant land, to regard it as one of our most urgent duties to increase in enthusiastic devotion to our Blessed Mother; I say enthusiastic, because all devotion to her which is not enthusiastic is simply unintelligent. In this matter coldness is the result of ignorance.

God has been unusually "rich in mercy" to the catholics of this country during late years. We cannot but feel that He has some specially gracious designs upon us, if only we correspond with an ardent humility to the outpouring of His grace. Among His recent blessings none has been more signal or more significant than the increase of devotion to our Blessed Lady amongst us. Her feasts are kept, not only with more ecclesiastical magnificence, which is of great importance, but also with more frequentation of the Sacraments, which is of greater importance. Her images are more frequent, and the kneelers around them more numerous and more fervent.

The preaching of Mary is now one of the prominent duties of the clergy. The increase of popular devotion, and so the vigour of popular faith, depends in no slight measure upon that preaching. According to the Litany, our Lady is the " Virgo prædicanda," " the Virgin to be preached," extolled, made much of, by the preachers of her Son. In a few more years the devotion to the grand Mother of God will have gone so far beyond what it is even now amongst us, that in the retrospect we shall hardly be able to understand how we could have been so backward so short a time ago.

I have said that devotion to our Blessed Lady developes most rapidly when the Church is in more than common tribulation. But the Venerable Grignon de Montfort tells us that its most remarkable developement is reserved for the last age of the Church, when her sufferings will have reached their height, and the triumph of the world will seem to be most complete. He tells us, from St. Vincent Ferrer, that God has reserved for those days saints of almost unparalleled grandeur, whose distinguishing characteristic will be their devouring zeal for Mary's honour, and who will enrich the persecuted Church with the new inventions of their fertile devotion. We may hail therefore

each new approved devotion to our Lady as
an augury or a shadow of the coming of those
latter times, and of the advent of those glorious saints. Is it lawful to conjecture that
foremost among them may be Elias himself,
who, in the extatic contemplations of his
mysterious earthly hiding-place, is nourishing
his supernatural life on the depths of the
Incarnation ? This has sometimes occurred
to me when I have been pondering on St.
Vincent's prediction. The prophet's vision
from the top of Carmel may well suggest the
thought.

Among the catholic devotions to our Blessed
Lady, which have of late been taking deeper
root in England, we may specify the Month
of Mary. This devotion is itself a visible
monument of that endless developement of
devotion to our Blessed Lady which char-
acterizes the life of the Church. It belongs
almost to our own times. St. Alphonso
Liguori, whom we may call our latest saint,
and who was himself one of the apostles of
Mary, does not seem to have known it. It
took its rise during the last century in the
Roman College under the auspices of Father
Muzzarelli the Jesuit ; but it does not appear
to have received authoritative sanction until
the present century. It has now become

part of the popular calendar of the Church. Although it is not recognized either in the Breviary or in the Missal, it has become as acknowledged a season of the Christian year as Advent or Lent. The Church has enriched it with Indulgences. Everywhere it is preached and celebrated as if it were a sort of annual mission to confirm, to perpetuate, to preserve, or to recover, the spiritual fruits of Lent. It comes in, like a privileged incursion, amongst the mysteries of Paschal-tide and Pentecost, taxing the skill of the pastor and the preacher to hinder its dislodging those mysteries from the minds and hearts of the faithful. It has thus become an excellent test of our loyal sympathy with the living Church. There is scarcely a Church or Oratory in Christendom which does not bear marks of this devotion. A Roman devotion, it spread, as the Raccolta tells us, through the Holy City first of all rather as a family devotion; and now, like all Roman things, it has overrun the world we can hardly tell how. Mary herself has consecrated and propagated it by miracles and graces, until it has become in these days one of the most prominent devotions of her children.

"Months of Mary" have been composed in almost all languages, and in endless varieties of form, matter, and intention, suitable to the

diversity of tastes in devotion. Each one
finds itself the favourite of some souls; and the
same souls in different years recreate themselves with different observances of our Lady's
Month. The "Month of Mary" now intro-
duced to the English reader has two peculiari-
ties, upon which a few words should be said.

There are some persons, who, in the practice of a devout life and in the pursuit of perfection, are not in any way consciously affected
by the spirit of modern times, or practically
aware of any peculiar difficulties which it
presents in the shape of temptations against
the faith or want of harmony with the old-
fashioned practices of the Church. If they are
studious or thoughtful persons they are quite
alive intellectually to the look of incongruity
with modern times which there is about the
almost unchanging Church, with its stern
theories of exclusive salvation, and its hopeless
attitude of resistance to the clamours of modern
political philosophy and the genius of so-called
progress. Intellectually, they appreciate
thoroughly the difficulties arising out of this
incongruity, and the apparent position of dis-
advantage in which it places catholics. But
practically it concerns them very little or not
at all. They take no interest in the matter,
further than that it is one of the million ways

in which the world kills souls. It does not trouble them in those inward lives of theirs which are "hidden with Christ in God." It drops off from them in their ascetical life. It looks to them as an insignificant and external matter, part of the weary burden which catholic journalists and controversialists must professionally bear, and a dispute in which the Church and the world can never understand each other, and to which therefore it is hopeless to expect any sort of conclusion whatever. Such men pray, and praise, and intercede, and mortify themselves, and occupy themselves with God, as if the nineteenth century were the third or the thirteenth. They are at peace. In their estimation truth cannot change, because the world changes, nor do theories become false because sin makes the practice of them impossible. They know that the end of the world is to be an irreconcileable complication of the Church and the world; and the gradual thickening and darkening of things towards this result, not being a matter of surprise to them, is also not a matter of disquietude.

But there are less fortunate souls upon whose inward life these difficulties prey like vultures. Their gift of faith is not strong enough to defend the cloister of their piety.

The world is a real difficulty to them. They
cannot so abstract themselves in the things of
God as not to hear the clamours of science,
politics, philosophy, and literature, calling
them every moment to account. To answer
objections to themselves must be part of their
piety, just as to answer objections to others
is part of their controversy. They cannot
give themselves up exclusively and without
further thought to the praise of God: because
they have got continually to prove to themselves His right to be praised. Hence their
spiritual life is neither the peace nor the
fruition which marks the spiritual life of the
former class. Such persons are to be pitied.
Yet they have God's work to do, and they
have their own way in which to serve Him.
For them also books must be provided, which,
even when they do not substantially answer
objections, console the reader by keeping the
objections in view, and speaking of them in
modern language. They who rebuilt the
walls of Jerusalem with the sword in one
hand and the trowel in the other, are the types
of these holy and afflicted souls. It seems to
be especially for them that this Book was
composed. It is redolent of a piety, which,
while it has its eyes fixed on the quietudes of
the eternal Throne never omits to see also

the disquietudes of unbelief. It implies perturbations by the very efforts which it makes to calm them. It is therefore very suitable for those who find that modern ways and modern thoughts and modern things penetrate into their inward lives, and make a noise there. It is no fault of theirs. It is a sorrow; and for all sorrows there is a consolation. Moreover it is a sorrow which may pass away; and these souls may one day win an entrance into a quieter and happier sanctuary.

The other characteristic of the Book before us is the way in which it is all based upon the single dogma of the Immaculate Conception. At this time it is plain that all devotion to our Blessed Lady must be deeply tinctured with this doctrine. Its recent Definition naturally becomes the very form of many devotions, and the presiding genius of all of them. But our Author has done far more than this in his Month of Mary. He has shown that this beautiful dogma has an especial mission to our own days, and is meant to be the peculiar apostle of our peculiar difficulties. It floods with new light those very relations of the human soul to God, which are just now so fertile of temptations against the faith. It satisfies doubts which are characteristically modern. It is before-

hand with some objections, and it imposes
silence upon others. It answers some difficulties by widening our field of vision, and so
showing in harmony and unity what we only
saw before fragmentarily and disjointedly.
It answers others by making them proofs of
divine truth instead of objections to it. It
helps us to understand God, and it helps us to
understand each other, and it helps us to
understand ourselves. Almost all modern
controversy can turn itself within the circle of
this glorious Dogma, and has room to fight
there as well as to turn, and to reach its
enemies without leaving its own defences.
All this has been brought out by the Author
of this Month of Mary, with a readiness which
is never unreal, and an ingenuity which is never
unnatural. Both these characteristics therefore, render his Book eminently a modern
Book, and suitable for those upon whom the
modern spirit imposes the painful trial of preserving the unction of their hearts in the
midst of the perplexity of their understandings.
God has many good servants and many dear
children amongst such persons: may He bless
them with an increase of love to His Immaculate Mother!

F. W. FABER.

THE MONTH OF MARY
CONCEIVED WITHOUT SIN.

MEDITATION I.

Lord, have mercy upon us; Christ, have mercy upon us;
Lord, have mercy upon us.

Lord, have mercy upon all men! Lord
Jesus, when Thou wert here, Thou hadst pity
on the world, and Thou didst shed tears when
Thou didst behold mankind all sitting in darkness and in death, all crushed under the weight
of evil, of suffering, and of sin.

Lord, let Thine eyes be ever upon us; let
Thy compassion never fail us. Look through
the world and see how many souls are dead!
Behold, how void of love men are, how void
of hope, and void of faith, and how in the
hopelessness of their hearts they make no
struggle, pour forth no prayer to Thee, but
bury themselves deeper and deeper in flesh
and blood. Behold, Lord, how these grovelling souls unman themselves, and become like
to beasts, how they spurn not Thy grace only,
but the natural use of their reason and their
freedom. Behold how men, in the mists of
sensuality and the madness of self-love, hate
each other, fear, betray, deceive and murder
one another, and, as the Prophet says, fill the

1

earth with adultery and with blood. (Osee iv. 2.) Behold, Lord, how the venom of sin ever spreads ruin among the nations, poisoning men's bodies and souls, their hearts and their minds.

Have mercy, Lord, on the multitudes of men who make no progress, upon whom no light has yet shone, whose darkness grows thicker day by day, the more they resist the influence of the true Sun that would fain enlighten their drowsy souls.

Have mercy on all Christian people! Have mercy on those who waver in their faith; who understand not the dignity of their calling, who know not the divine power that dwells within them, nor the virtues that cleanse and the doctrines that heal us, which Thou bestowest on all men through Thy Church! Have pity on those who, through tepidity, hesitate and stop short, for whom that dreadful hour of the Apocalypse seems to have struck, when the King of men, disgusted as it were, and wearied out with waiting, casts them off, and vomits them out of His heart. (Apoc. iii. 16.)

Have mercy, Lord, on all who truly seek to find Thee, and who endeavour more and more to conform their thoughts, their conduct, and their laws, to Thy divine Word. Have mercy on the hard struggles they have to make against hypocrisy and ignorance, against the spirit of evil, against those who would corrupt the world!

Have mercy on those separated Christians who are beginning to have a glimpse of the pure light of Catholicity, but who, without Thine aid, will long remain under the yoke of established falsehood, of ignorance well nigh invincible, of the love of their rich endowments, and of inveterate hatred against the central authority of Thy Church! Above all, Lord, have mercy on all faithful souls who are striving against sin! Have mercy on those souls who, with Saint Paul, constantly pray to be delivered; and to whom Thou dost answer: "Fight on, my grace is sufficient for you." (2 Cor. xii. 9.) Ah! Lord, how long shall we be always falling into sin, after a few short struggles, after some slight victories? How long shall we be forced to say: "My sin is ever before me?" (Ps. l. 5.) How long shall our faces be covered with confusion? How long shall the sight of the light, and the love of life only lead to more cruel struggles with darkness and death? How long shall we lack that progress which makes the grain of mustard seed grow into the great tree to which all the heavenly virtues are gathered together? How long shall we lack that divine growth, without which no one can either serve Thee, or fight under Thy banner for the good of men? How long, O my God, shall all those souls whom Thou dost call to sanctity, waste their strength in this dark conflict with evil? O Lord, have mercy on us!

Lord, have mercy on all men in every necessity of mind or body. Have mercy on all new-born babes who are in danger of dying unbaptized. Have mercy on the babes destined to be thrown into the rivers, or into the streets, for the dogs to eat !

Have mercy on those, the very gates of whose life are hemmed in and surrounded with vice! Have mercy on the child who is falling upon its first scandal! Have mercy on youth in the age of passion, when the first excitement of the senses slays the souls of half their number, even as in the natural order, half the infants that are born die within a year of their birth !

Have mercy on those whose minds are so open to scandal, at the age when the sophisms of ignorance so easily warp us from the truth !

Have mercy on the young girls, whom poverty has brought to despair, and on those who are intoxicated with pleasure.

Have mercy on those who, when they come to the full use of reason and of liberty, hesitate between the path of pleasure and that of justice and truth ! Have mercy on those who begin, and then turn back. Have mercy too on those who begin and go on valiantly for half a life, and in middle age get weary, look behind them, and ask back from the earth the tinsel prizes which, in the purity of their youth they had been wise enough to despise.

Have mercy on the infirm and aged, whose weakness casts a sickly hue on all things, to whom blindness and palsy leave no other thought than the barren and monotonous care of their poor remains of life.

Have mercy on the dying, who have come to their last hour, and yet have not begun the labour of their life, nor planted in their heart the seed of eternal life!

———

MEDITATION II.

Christ, hear us! Christ, graciously hear us. God, the Father of heaven, have mercy on us! God the Son, Redeemer of the world, have mercy on us! God the Holy Ghost, have mercy on us Holy Trinity, one God, have mercy on us.

Lord, our evils are great; sin is the only real evil, and the spring of its bitter waters is never dry. In the individual soul it seems to multiply with its years, and in each nation with its progress. Nevertheless the Holy Church ceases not to pray: Hear us, graciously hear us, deliver us from evil!

Will evil never be lessened among us? Will Thy kingdom never come upon earth, as it is in heaven? Shall God and His Christ never be better known? Shall Thy Gospel never bring nations and hearts under its sway more than now? Shall the nations of the world never be healed, or shall they never become less blind to Thy truth? Shall not the number of Thy servants and friends, Thy worshippers in spirit and truth, be multiplied among men? Shall every one that cometh into the world find himself surrounded by the same darkness, the same stumbling-blocks? Let it not be, we beseech Thee; Lord, hear our prayer.

Lord, hear the prayers which Thy Holy Spirit inspires, and which we offer to Thee on behalf of all mankind: " God of my fathers, and Lord of mercy, who hast made all things with Thy word, and by Thy wisdom hast appointed man that he should have dominion over the creature that was made by Thee, that he should order the world according to equity and justice, and execute justice with an upright heart; give us wisdom, that sitteth by Thy throne, and cast us not off." (Wisdom ix. 1.)

Can this prayer be made in vain? Shall not wisdom be given to us? Shall man, who was born to have dominion over all created things, remain for ever slavishly bound to them by his senses? Shall man, who was born to order and dispose the world in justice and equity, shall he never cease polluting it with adultery and blood, with rapine and iniquity? Is there no remedy for all this evil?

Lord, when Thy children are encouraged to believe that the time is drawing near when Thou shalt come again to reign on the earth, shall they be deceived in their hope?* Shall we say that the pious belief now so general throughout the Church, that Thou wilt renew the earth in the knowledge and love of Jesus, by the union of hearts with the heart of Mary Immaculate,† is false? Didst not Thou Thyself, O Lord, inspire the hearts of Thy faithful and of their pastors with this same hope, by that mysterious operation of the Holy Spirit, which the holy Fathers speak of?

---

* Cat. Con. Trid. on the words, "Thy kingdom come."

† See Petavius, *de Incar.* lib. 14. c. 3. no. 10. &c.; and Passagia *de Immac,* p. 10.

Let us persevere in our prayer, let us ask God to give us the knowledge and the practice of those remedies which He has prepared for us. In the spirit of faith let us invoke the Father, the Son, and the Holy Ghost.

Father, Creator of the world, have mercy on the work of Thy hands. Thou didst foresee all the consequences of the abuse of free will; sin, disobedience, pride, self-love, and all evil desires; Thou didst foresee all our sufferings and death; but Thou didst also foresee, and didst prepare a remedy, and man himself was its treasure-house. Thou didst give him treasures of hidden strength for his life-long strife with Satan. O Father of heaven, display all these treasures, and employ all this force.

Son, Redeemer of the world, who by Thine own infinite power hast restored that which no created power could have raised up, who by Thy boundless love hast been pleased to make Thyself one with the work of Thine hands, to save him, to deliver him from evil, and to bring him one day to the enjoyment of eternal perfection; Thou who didst so love purity that none but a virgin could give Thee birth, and who didst so love sanctity that Thou didst preservo Thy Virgin Mother from all stain of original sin; who didst thus reserve for Thyself in the midst of a fallen world one spot of immaculate purity, there to unite Thyself with human nature; Thou who by Thy labours, Thy virtues, Thy sufferings, agony, and infinite merits, hast remedied the irreparable wrongs of sin; who, finally, by Thy death and sacrifice hast opened to men the living source of life eternal—O God the Son, Redeemer of the world, continue the work of our redemption, pour forth Thy merits, sanctify Thy Church, increase the number of labourers, and of those who follow Thee; give zeal to those who are to fight Thy battles, who suffer and conquer with Thee, to whom Thou hast promised that they shall do greater works even than Thine!

Holy Spirit, Sanctifier of the world, Love eternal and infinite; Love who art in God and who art God; Love whose fire sanctifies; Thou who didst impart to Mary ever Virgin, her divine and supernatural maternity; and by whose operation that crowning fruit which God, from all eternity, designed His works to produce, was born; Thou who wouldst begin Thy new creation by making an immaculate heart, to be the one refuge for God in the midst of universal wickedness,—Holy Spirit, have mercy on us! Console us in this valley of tears! Dissipate our darkness, drive away our enemies, shed forth Thy light, inflame our hearts, " create"* Thine elect, " renew the face of the earth," keep up the succession of doctors and saints; increase in us the gifts of knowledge and of piety; so may we hope for the coming of the kingdom of God on earth. Thou didst reveal truths to the Apostles, such as they could not bear while Jesus was yet on the earth; they are in the keeping of Thy Church; but how little do the Church's chil-

* Ps. ciii. 30.

dren know of the treasures of science contained in divine truth! Often have the Fathers of the Church grieved, with St. Paul, that they could not impart to the feeble the "bread of the strong!" A servant of God wrote more than a century ago: "Till now Mary has been unknown, and this is one reason why Jesus Christ is not known as He should be. If then, as no one can doubt, the reign of Jesus Christ is coming upon the earth, it will be but a necessary consequence of the knowledge of the most Holy Virgin and of her reign in men's hearts."* Oh my God, how these words of Thy servant transport me with joy! It may be that the definition of the Immaculate Conception of Mary, with all the consequences which it involves, will shed a new lustre on the most fundamental truths of faith. Spirit of light, shorten the days of our spiritual infancy, and by Thy holy inspirations, show forth in the church, and in our souls, the full light of Thy divine word.†

Holy Trinity, one God, have mercy on us! Grant that in us may be accomplished ever more and more, that last prayer of Jesus Christ, "That they may be one, as we are one." (John xvii. 2.) All the innumerable multitudes of men now dwelling on the earth, all who have lived and all who are yet to live,— Thou didst create them to have but one heart and one soul, to be one as Thou art, to be one

* Treatise on true devotion to the Blessed Virgin, by F. de Montfort, p. 7.

† Spiritus tuus inducat nos in omnen, sicut tuus promisit Filius, veritatem.—Miss. Rom. in præpar. ad Missam.

amongst themselves and with Thee. But all have forsaken Thee; they have fallen from Thee, who art their true centre, and are scattered till no two remain together. Two or three gathered together in Thy name, O God, are such a wonder, that Thou dost promise them, whenever they can be found, to dwell in the midst of them, and to grant them whatsoever they ask Thee. (Matt. xviii. 19.) O Holy Trinity, Father, Son, and Holy Ghost, One God, and pattern of our unity, have mercy upon us! Take away all hindrances to our unity! Bring to pass the triumph of that kingdom, that city whose members are at unity among themselves. (Ps. cxxi. 3.) Gather up according to the prayer of one of Thy servants each soul into unity with itself, and all souls into the catholic unity of our mother the heavenly Jerusalem. She is the mother of all men that are collected into the one Church, the queen of unity, the ark of the covenant, outside which no man can be in Thee, O God, Thou uncreated Centre of all spirits, and of all flesh. May this gate of heaven be opened wider and wider for mankind to pass in, and to be united to Thee!

MEDITATION III.

Holy Mary, pray for us! Holy Mother of God, pray for us!

And where shall we find this refuge of mankind? Where is this wisdom who is the treasure house of Thy strength, O my God, through whom evil may be overcome and destroyed, and whose power can draw Thee down into the hearts of all mankind? Where is this one undefiled spot of Thy creation through which Thou couldst come back into the world? Where is this heart of mankind into which the Word came down to take flesh amongst us, on which the Holy Spirit was shed for the work of our new creation? Who is this Mother of regenerate man, this Queen of unity, this Gate of heaven, by whom mankind is at unity with itself and with God? Who is she but that Queen of heaven whom the Church has named Mother of God? In the midst of the holy city of Jerusalem, which is the Church of God, and the house of unity, is the Ark of the Covenant, the Queen of Unity, the Mother of divine Love, the Mother of Mankind, and of the Church herself; who is, with and after Jesus Christ, the centre of the world of spirits; who is, with and after the Holy Ghost, the heart of the city of God; this centre, this heart, is the Holy Mother of God.

O Mary, Mother of God, pray for us! Obtain for us now the grace to meditate with understanding and with love, upon the mystery of Thine office, a mystery, the daily increasing manifestation of whose reality, splendour, and power, is perhaps the refuge which God has reserved for these latter days.

Truly Thou, O God, art the refuge of the world; Thou only, O Jesus, our Redeemer, art the world's Salvation. But the world will not be saved if it rejects God and His Christ,

counsels it was decreed that our nature should be associated with God in the work of redemption, and if God willed to become Son of Man, He willed also, that one human person, in the name of all mankind, should consent to become Mother of God.*

Thou then, O Holy Mother of God, art the refuge of us men, for by thee God entered into the world, and will enter more and more into each soul, and into all mankind. Through thee every soul may always hope to be a saint; through thee, the nations that God made for health, may, if they will, be healed; by thee, the world, still so full of lawlessness and darkness, may advance in the road of light and equity.

Holy Mother of God, from all eternity God willed to unite Himself with His creature, that He might draw it towards Himself. But He needed thy birth, thy worth, thy merits, and thy consent, before He could accomplish His eternal purpose. Well, then, mayest thou be called the Mother of the new creation and of the world to come.

God is always full of love, and all that He desires is to enter the soul of every man; He knocks at the door of the heart, and waits for it to be opened to Him; He is always there, but we are almost always away. He will not enter before we return, before we enter into

---

* St. Thomas says "It was fitting that it should be announced to the Blessed Virgin that she was to conceive Christ....in order to show that there was a kind of spiritual marriage between the Son of God and human nature. And therefore, through the annunciation, the consent of the Blessed Virgin, in lieu of that of all human nature, was asked for." Sum. 3. q. 30. art. 1.

if mankind refuses to co-operate in the work of its salvation. The grace of God ever knocks at our door, but we are ever free to reject it; we must say with St. Augustine, "O my God, Thou hast created us by Thyself, without our aid, but Thou savest us not without our consent." There is then, as it were, a human side to redemption, and man must co-operate with God. "We are," says St. Paul, "fellow-workers with God." (1 Cor. iii. 9.)

God begins, man must continue; God gives, and man must take; God speaks, and man must listen; God enlightens and inspires, man must understand and obey.

And of these two forces, God's which works our redemption, and man's which co-operates for our redemption, which is the defaulter? Does God fail us, or do we fail God?

From the beginning to the end of history, man has ever been wanting to God—God has never been wanting to man. "God," says St. Thomas, (2da. 2dæ. q. iv. art. 4. ad 3.) "is ever working man's justification, as the sun ever operating the illumination of the air." The backwardness of the world, the wounds of our nature, the falling away of nations, the apostasies of men, are due only to us; and since Christ died to save us, since He left us His Sacraments to renew us, since He sent the Holy Spirit to dwell in His Church, our victory, our progress, our eternal salvation, depend in some sort upon ourselves, and are in our own hands.

In one essential point, redemption has always depended upon man. In the eternal

counsels it was decreed that our nature should
be associated with God in the work of redemption, and if God willed to become Son
of Man, He willed also, that one human person, in the name of all mankind, should consent to become Mother of God.*

Thou then, O Holy Mother of God, art the
refuge of us men, for by thee God entered
into the world, and will enter more and more
into each soul, and into all mankind. Through
thee every soul may always hope to be a saint;
through thee, the nations that God made for
health, may, if they will, be healed; by thee,
the world, still so full of lawlessness and darkness, may advance in the road of light and
equity.

Holy Mother of God, from all eternity God
willed to unite Himself with His creature,
that He might draw it towards Himself. But
He needed thy birth, thy worth, thy merits,
and thy consent, before He could accomplish
His eternal purpose. Well, then, mayest thou
be called the Mother of the new creation and
of the world to come.

God is always full of love, and all that He
desires is to enter the soul of every man; He
knocks at the door of the heart, and waits for
it to be opened to Him; He is always there,
but we are almost always away. He will not
enter before we return, before we enter into

* St. Thomas says "It was fitting that it should be announced
to the Blessed Virgin that she was to conceive Christ....In order
to show that there was a kind of spiritual marriage between the
Son of God and human nature. And therefore, through the
annunciation, the consent of the Blessed Virgin, in lieu of that
of all human nature, was asked for." Sum. 3. q. 30. art. 1.

our heart, where He wishes to dwell. He
will not be born within us until thou art
with us, O Mary, until thou hast communi-
cated to us in some sort the virtue of thy
divine maternity, the blessed state of those of
whom Jesus said, " Whosoever doeth the will
of my Father who is in heaven, he is my
mother." (Matt. xii. 50.)   It is, then, through
thy intercession, and through imitation of thee,
that each soul arrives at its everlasting end.

So also, O Mother of God, though God is
always present with His Church, to inspire
her and to rule her, nevertheless there are
periods when the triumphs of the Church are
few, and there are others when they abound.
Sometimes schisms divide her, and heresies
weaken her ; sometimes brilliant victories
strengthen her ; schisms come to an end, and
whole nations are restored to her fold.   Has
man no share in all these changes ?   His
prayer which draws down God, his meritorious
actions which make God take up His abode on
earth, the good use of his free-will, thy intercession, which he invokes more or less ardently, thy example, more or less closely followed,
these are the means of enlarging the kingdom
of God, and of multiplying the triumphs of the
Church.

God is willing to give us all; all now depends on us, and on thee, by whom all is
received and treasured up, by whom all is
transmitted, O Mother of God !   All depends on
the union of men with her who receives all
from God.

O Mary, holy Mother of God, obtain for me

that I may know and meditate upon these truths, for the sole purpose of applying them to my soul, and framing my life by them. Let me not be contented with a speculative knowledge which leads not to love, and is not true to itself.

O my God! at least once in my life may I say with Thy prophet, "Now have I begun; this is the change of the right hand of the Most High." (Ps. lxxvi. 11.) How often have I begun and not gone on! When shall I begin in earnest? When shall I experience that new life and that lasting change which God alone can work?

Oh Virgin, Mother of God, there never was any true change, any true renewal of the world, but through thee! "God has created a new thing upon the earth," (Jerm. xxx. 22.) says the prophet, in proclaiming thy divine maternity. Yes, I see, there never was a new thing in the world, till He whose name is *God-with-us* came into it. There never will be new life in me, until the Eternal Word is born in my soul. Hath He not said, My Mother is he who doeth the will of God? My soul, therefore, must in a sense become mother of God, because she must do the will of God. God wills to exalt my soul to this heavenly state, but I, like thee, O Mother of God, must merit it by His grace. Help me, then, while I strive to merit the increase of the new life and the birth of the new man; which the Holy Ghost seeks to create in me, and whose germ the Holy Communion plants in my soul. Under thy fostering hand may this germ grow into a tree of life. Let not the floods of vulgar cares too soon wash away the body, the blood, and the soul of Jesus thy Son, when He has come to me; may mortal sin never again crucify the new man in me, may the blight of perpetual venial sins no longer stint His growth and hold Him captive; may the time come quickly for grace to triumph in my soul, and for the Truth to declare that Jesus grows therein in grace and wisdom before God and man.

MEDITATION IV.

Mother of divine grace, pray for us

Mother of divine grace, pray for us! Thou who hast received all grace, thou who hast conceived in thy womb the fountain-head of grace, who art filled with grace that thou mayest impart it to us,* O Mother of Grace, pray that we may know the merit of thy maternity; pray that we may share it, that the grace of God may no more fall fruitlessly on us or on the world, that we may no longer choke its growth, or refuse it, as the glaciers or the sands of the desert which feel not the fertilizing influences of the sun.

He who doth the will of my Father, says our Saviour, is my brother, my sister, and *my mother.* Doing God's will is the condition of the soul's becoming a mother of grace; and

---

* Omnium divinarum gratiarum sedem.—Bull of Pius IX.

the peerless Virgin, who ever perfectly accomplished the will of God, thereby merited to conceive grace in Its fulness, and in Its fountain-head. From the first moment of her life she was obedient to all the most secret and the most imperceptible inspirations of grace. She was obedient all through her life, and never ceased to watch, like the best of mothers, over the infant Saviour. She was obedient, we may be sure, to death, even to the death of the cross ; for she suffered in the sight of her Son on the cross all that He suffered, and her will was united to God's in willing all the sufferings that He felt, and that she felt with Him.

God's grace is like the sun, it shines on the good and on the evil; but the good obey, and answer to the inspirations of grace, and their souls acquire some of the marks of a divine maternity that conceives and develops the seeds of grace; the bad remain barren.

This is the whole secret of Christian life, and of the progress of each soul, and of the world. God begins, but man must follow and obey, must act and must suffer that he may in some sort deserve to partake of the holy maternity of grace.

In the history of the spiritual life, the first period is the day of miracles and of great consolations; the latter days should be the seasons of great and austere virtues. The first period is that of our mercenary life, when God gives all and man returns little ; the latter times are those of sacrifice, when man, more advanced, seeks to make greater returns to God. The soul that would experience nothing but miracles and consolations, is one that does not persevere, and that never progresses.

It seems that when a soul is newly born to grace, God at first undertakes to bear it as a mother carries her child ; He Himself moves its limbs for it, and fills its youth with a holy joy, and with abundance of strength.   But man, like the prodigal son, soon exhausts the store, which ever grows less till the fatal moment when all his warmth, all his energy is spent ; and at the very time when he should be beginning to make some returns, to go alone, and to support himself, like a child who has learned to walk, to go freely to God by the way of sacrifice, then he first begins to feel his weakness, his poverty, his powerlessness in the struggle against sin.. Then it is that souls, which seemed given up to God, but which in the midst of His unceasing graces, still lived immersed in flesh and blood, and only sought God with reservations and with conditions, then it is that such souls have a sudden fall, and, after seeming to have their conversation in heaven, by a shocking catastrophe are found wallowing in the mud like Solomon, and finish with the flesh, after they had begun with the spirit. (Galat. iii. 3.) This is what Scripture means when it says, " The bloody and deceitful men shall not live out half their days." (Ps. liv. 24.)   For after a promising spring, which gives blossoms in abundance, many a soul never reaches the season of maturity, when she should bear fruit and yield her harvest to God.   In spite of the fair promise, the canker-worm was gnawing at the root of these blooming trees; legions of invisible insects were poisoning the flowers and the seed; the storms of earth had destroyed the hopes of the year, and the springtide promise of the richest gifts of heaven ended in abortion and barrenness.

Thus the fount of concupiscence, of pride, and sensuality, which we bear within us at our birth, often continues its work. in souls which have received the most sublime inspirations and the greatest gifts of grace; and it man, by the strictest watchfulness, the most exact and humble obedience, the most determined conflict, and by a sacrifice of self to God, as complete as that of God for us—if man, in proportion to the greatness of the gifts he has received, will not in his turn give himself, humble himself, and sacrifice himself, the soul also will have her overwhelming storms and her consuming fires, will have her hidden leprosy, and her legions of invisible enemies, who will surely compass her fall on her way through this life, and will bring her empty and barren before the tribunal of God.

O thou, Mother of Grace, and Mother of Souls, in whom no concupiscence could ever grow, for it had no root in thee, pray for us, and preserve our souls from the awful curse of barrenness. Thou didst co-operate with every grace;—obtain then for us, that according to our poor measure we may correspond with God's endeavours to save us; that the human side in the work of our salvation may not be false to the divine side, and that when the

time comes for the soul to act with God and
to follow Him, to answer His calls, to pay
back what He has lent, to ripen the fruits
which He has sown and quickened, the soul
may be found fruitful, and may not be cursed
like the barren fig-tree, on which Jesus sought
fruit and found none.

O Mother of Grace, I would now begin to
act and to suffer that I may escape the curse
of final barrenness. I now see that at all
times God stirs me up with His grace, and
tries to rouse me from my sleep and my sloth.
Has He not often said to me, as He did to the
paralytic of the Gospel, "Rise up, and walk,"
and I have not walked? Every day He tries
to wake me out of my slumbers, but I only
sleep on. As every morning the Father of
the world awakens men, rouses them. from
their bodily sleep, and commands them to rise
and go to their daily toil, so it is in the life
of my soul. "Watch and pray; rise up and
walk; take the cross and follow me;" these
are the words which I hear. It is the voice
of Him whom St. Augustine calls the "Father
of the morning watch."

But who awakes to the true life, who
wakes to work with God? Who learns to
walk with perseverance? Who will bear His
cross? I will, O Mother of Grace. I have
delayed too long, I have slept overmuch. Time
flies. The time which God has allotted to my
earthly sojourn will all be spent if I do not
now awake.

MEDITATION V.

Help of Christians, pray for us!

Help of Christians, pray for us! Pray that Christian nations may fulfil their destiny on the earth!

Neither mankind nor men are forced into good or evil. Mankind is free, it can make a choice. Its end will be good or bad, as it pleases.

It is the same with the world at large as with each man. One man passes from the grace and purity of childhood, to the consuming fire of youth, "and rooteth up all things that spring." (Job, xxxi. 12.) Then, as years go on, ambition and avarice harden his heart, till the moral blindness of self-love comes upon him and he sinks into a vicious and unhappy old age. Another passes from his tender age to the bright ardour of generous youth; and after worthily spending the strength of his manhood, enjoys the calm autumnal days of a good old age, and awaits the time of his departure like a wise man full of goodness, love, and piety.

Mankind, here on earth, can choose between these two paths. Any one may become wise or a fool, a saint or a sinner, as he wills.

There is in the mind of God an ideal plan of history which would be the best to follow, but which man by his disobedience, may change; and in His mind there is also a plan for the life of each man. But few men follow out the plan of their heavenly vocation. In this divine plan there is an order of days, of periods of progress, such as God would have it; but the Holy Scripture tells us: "Bloody and deceitful men shall not live out half their days." So it is with all mankind. They may live on in the perversity of their flesh and blood, but their end will be evil, they will not fulfil the second part of their history according to the plan which God prefers.

As there is a crisis in each man's life, so there is a crisis in the world's history. "In the midst of my days I shall go to the gates of hell:" says the prophet, (Is. xxxviii. 10.) "O Lord, Thy work, in the midst of the years bring it to life." (Habac. iii. 1.) This is the prayer which all mankind and each man should address to God through her who is the help of Christians, if we would in the end escape the curse of sterility and reap the harvest of our labours.

And what is the great crisis now going on in the world? May not the seed which well-nigh sixty centuries have sown, have come to maturity? May not this be the time for the harvest of men which we are to witness? Such may be, perhaps, the question proposed to the human race in these our days.

Listen to the divine words which the Saviour taught us, which are and ought to be the constant prayer of every wise man: "Our Father, who art in heaven, Thy kingdom come, Thy will be done on earth as it is in heaven." What do they mean? They mean, that there is a kingdom of God on earth, for the coming

of which we ought to pray ; which man's perversity may retard or put an end to, in each
soul and throughout the world, and whose
coming is the fulfilment of the Will of God on
earth as it is in heaven.

It may be that all depends on the free choice
of the age in which we live. If the men of this
age declare themselves more decidedly for and
against God ; if too many minds remain rooted
in hatred and in credulity ; if Christians are
tepid and weak, and too often fall into sin ;
if they rouse themselves not by some great act .
of faith, by some generous impulse towards
truth, by stronger habits of hope and charity,
then may these years of grace and trial prove
our last, the world end ill, and die in a rapid
decay, before the kingdom of God can be
increased and before its fruits can come to maturity.

Who but man then would be the cause of
this premature death ? And who but man can
avert it, by corresponding to the grace of
God ? For the grace of God abounds, but our
co-operation fails. Life is in our own hands :
do we desire it ? God has given Himself :
shall we receive Him ? If there is one thing
after which all men should strive, it is this :
to know God, to receive the Saviour, and to
accept the grace which is offered or given to
us. But this has been already done by one
among the children of men, by the Virgin
Mary, Mother of God, Mother of grace, Mother
of the Saviour. By her free consent, God was
born into the world and made one of us ; by
her free consent, Jesus was offered for the sal-

vation of the world. What then remains to be done?. That all the world, and each soul in the world, should be united with her who co-operated in the redemption, and is the help of Christians, that they should take her for their model, for their guide, their queen, and their Mother, in order that with·her and like her, they may receive the Redeemer and establish His reign on earth as it is in heaven.

Would that those of our separated brethren who do not know the Blessed Virgin, nor what is signified by her, nor why the Catholic Church is always adding to the homage of love which she pays her, might comprehend that she co-operated of her own free will in the work of salvation, and that she represents, with and after Jesus Christ, the free co-operation o man with God. She received God in all His fulness, she obeyed, she acted and suffered freely, knowingly and perfectly, for the salvation of the world, and in so doing she represents the human element in the work of the salvation of man. She is the representative of that reason and liberty in the presence of God, which He inspires and aids; she says to God: "Behold the handmaid of the Lord." Jesus Christ is the God-Man; but Mary is human nature pure and simple in the presence of God and of His Christ, seeking after God with all its strength, with all its mind, and all its heart.

If then there is any one point in religion on which, after the Man-God, all depends, it is the Blessed Virgin and true devotion to her. It was God's will to give Himself to man; it

was her will that received Him; and now that
Jesus Christ continues to bestow Himself upon
us, it is by the Blessed Virgin, by her worship,
by the thought of her, by imitating her, by her
intercession, that we shall likewise receive Him
and accept His kingdom. The redemption
has been accomplished, it has only to be applied. If then there is any question of the
progress of the kingdom of God upon earth, it
is surely chiefly on our side. The question is,
what will be our courage, our ardour, our
fidelity in walking in the footsteps of the Queen
of men, the Mother of grace, the co-operator
in our salvation, and the help of Christians?
If then among the manifold characteristics of
Christian piety, there is one of greater efficacy,
one which is stronger, more glorious, more
noble, more manly than any other, more worthy of man in the fulness of his strength, his
reason, and his liberty, it is that which adheres
most closely to the spirit of the Blessed Virgin,
to the imitation of her spirit, which consists in
desiring to work with God, by means of obedience, labour, courage, and sacrifices, that we
may merit an increase of His kingdom both in
ourselves and in all men.

I resolve then, O my God, to cultivate this
pure and virginal spirit, which alone is worthy
to receive Thee, and alone can give fruitfulness to the soul. I desire, like the Mother of
Grace, to work for God. And in order to
imitate Jesus Christ, and to become also His
Mother,* I desire to co-operate by my labours

* "For whosoever shall do the will of My Father that is in

2

and sacrifices towards my own salvation and
that of the whole world, as the Holy Scripture
says of the Machabees, who in the holy enthusiasm of their courage, " did not care to save
themselves alone, but undertook to save the
greatest possible number of their brethren."
I will not forget that mankind needs the efforts
of all its children, that the extension of God's
kingdom on earth may be arrested by my
crimes, and that if the issue of the struggle, in
this critical epoch of the world, is uncertain,
each one may do something towards defeat or
victory.

O Mary, Queen of men, through whom God
came upon earth, and there took flesh ; whom
God created without spot, that through thee
eternal light * might shine over the world ;
whom God made fruitful through thine immaculate purity ; who didst undertake the human
side of salvation in union with the humanity of
Jesus Christ, when thou didst speak the words;
" Behold the handmaid of the Lord, be it done
unto me according to Thy word"—O Queen
of mankind, Mother of divine grace, and Help
of Christians, if we are now in the midst of
that crisis which is to determine and decide
the destiny of mankind upon earth, now is the
time to manifest and put forth all the power
God hath given thee.

heaven, he is my brother, and sister, and mother." (Matt. xii.
50.) See also the IXth lesson in the Office of the Blessed Virgin
in the Roman Breviary.

* Quæ lumen æternum mundo effudit J. C. D. N. (Preface
of the Mass of the B. Virg.)

MEDITATION VI.

Queen, conceived without sin, pray for us

O Queen of men, pray that we may come to know what is that progress of·Christian wisdom, which is wanted in this present time of trial to secure the future interests of mankind upon earth.

In Rome there may be seen a humble sanctuary, the home for the last century of the body of the Blessed Leonard of Port-Maurice. By the side of the body there is an autograph letter of the holy man, which is also exposed to the veneration of the faithful. It contains an answer to the questions which we are now seeking to clear up. The contents are startling, but the traces of heavenly illumination and divine inspiration are discernible. It speaks of the mystery of the Immaculate Conception, and declares that when the light of that fundamental truth shall shine forth in all its splendour, then will come the hour for the repose and peace of the world ; but that, until that time, " we must pray and suffer, and be content to see the world in its present state of confusion."

Blessed Leonard further declares, that this light shall shine abroad after the Church has defined the dogma of the Immaculate Conception to be an article of faith. The prophecy may turn out untrue, but it contains an element of truth to which our hearts should cling with faith and love; I mean the principle which is

the foundation of the holy man's pious con-
victions, namely, that the world is not to remain for ever in its present state of confusion;
that man is destined to order the world in
peace, justice, and truth; that the progress
of Christian wisdom will bring rest to the
earth; and that this progress will consist in
bringing to light, applying, and fully developing the mystery of Mary, which is also the
mystery of human nature, and the whole glorious extent of the merits and of the dignity of
the Immaculate Virgin, Mother of the Incarnate
Word.

O Queen, conceived without sin, pray for
us! Pray, that in these our days the manifestation of this mystery may become a shining light in thy Church. Pray that this
manifestation may be such a progress of Christian wisdom as S. Vincent of Lerins speaks of
in the same pages which warn the Christians
of his days against dangerous novelties. "Shall
there never be," he exclaims, "any religious
progress in the Church of Christ? Assuredly
there shall be very great progress. And who
would be so envious of man, so hostile to God,
as to wish to hinder it? Yes, there shall be
progress in the faith, but no change in the
faith; let then understanding, knowledge, and
wisdom, grow and develop from age to age,
both in the universal Church, and in the individual soul. In the course of time, the old
doctrines of the heavenly philosophy must be
more and more cultivated and explained, they
can never be changed, maimed, or mutilated,
but they must acquire more clearness, evidence

and precision, while they preserve the fulness, integrity and propriety, that they originally possessed."*

"Yes," says another learned theologian, " we must think of the mystical body of Jesus Christ as we think of His natural body. Scripture says that as He increased in age, He grew also in wisdom and in grace. It was not that the eternal wisdom of God, even when clothed in our flesh, could increase in knowledge or in holiness, but in condescension to the laws of our nature, He exhibited day by day, more wisdom and more piety, as He grew in age, although from the first moment of His conception He had been perfect Wisdom and perfect holiness. So it is in a manner in the Church ; she brought forth from time to time the treasures of her tradition, and brought to light points of doctrine and practices of devotion, which had not hitherto cropped out, because the season had not come to exhibit them, nor to develop their ancient traditions. The fulness of the Holy Ghost resides, and from the beginning has resided, in the heart of the Church, but she only exhibits herself in external action, according to the counsels of eternal Providence, which guides our whole race as if it were a single individual, and each individual as if he were all mankind, through the various stages of life."†

O Mary, conceived without sin, pray that in this season of darkness and discouragement

---

* Passage quoted in the Bull of Pius IX.
† Thomassin, Treatise on the Feasts of the Church, Book II. c. 9.

some such splendid development of Christian wisdom and knowledge may flash upon us, and give fresh heart to those who do believe, and fresh good-will to those who would believe.

But if there is a point to which modern developments must tend, it is doubtless the mystery of Mary, and not the mystery of the Word—the mystery of man, not the mystery of God. "There are many reasons," says a pious author, "why God willed that the mystery of Mary should dawn by degrees like the day; which, in its first faint glimmer begins to disperse the gloom, till the sunrise bursts forth into the full blaze of light. One reason, as theologians commonly say, is this: because the Church is not founded on our Lady, but upon her Son; therefore it was convenient that God should first make clear the truths of salvation, and afterwards in the superabundance of His goodness, should clear up others, which, though of less consequence, yet raise our minds to know Him better and to love Him more ardently."

O Mary, Queen conceived without sin, pray that a glimpse may be given to us, of the possibility at least, of this glorious development of the kingdom of God upon earth.

The Immaculate Conception of the Virgin is a truth so deep, so fundamental, and so central,—it throws so strong a light on all the truths of faith, and even on all the truths of philosophy, that its fuller manifestation will perhaps contribute to bring about that intellectual revolution in the Christian world, and in the human mind, which clear-sighted souls are looking for.

This intellectual revolution may give to Europe a new age of faith, of light, and of unity. Once united, the nations of Europe might soon convert the whole world to the Gospel; it would be the grandest epoch of history, it would be the manifest coming of the kingdom of Jesus Christ; it will be the beginning, perhaps, of a series of ages, like those announced by S. John, the beloved disciple, after he had seen the "great sign" which appeared in heaven. "The woman, clothed with the sun, and crowned with stars"—"I saw an angel coming down from heaven, with a great chain in his hand, and he laid hold on the spirit of error, the old serpent, to bind him for a thousand years, that he should no more seduce the nations." (Apoc. xx. 1-3.)

O Mary, Queen conceived without sin, may we not hope that this clear announcement of the dogma of thine absolute purity may announce to us the time of thy final victory over all heresies?—that time when the angel, with the unbroken chain of truths in his hands, shall bind for many a long year the spirit of error, which seduces whole nations.

O my God, if I had real belief that my prayers and my works could contribute to the progress of the Christian truth upon earth; if I believed that I might add my mite to that mighty attraction by which Thou wouldest draw the world out of its degradation and raise it to justice, light and peace;—I feel that such

a faith would rouse me from my slumbers.
Poor and weak as I am, I would give the little
that I have, I would do the little that I can.
I would give myself entirely for the truth.　I
would live and die to obtain a ray of light the
more for this benighted world.

———

MEDITATION VII.

Queen, conceived without sin, pray for us.

What, then, is the mystery of Mary ? and
what her immaculate conception?

A few comparisons may help us to understand the question.

Mankind is a single organised body, a whole,
which, though made up of so many multitudes,
yet before God has in one sense but one
heart, one soul, one blood. From the moment that sin first infected the whole mass,
and plunged it into the abyss of self-love and
concupiscence, God willed to prepare for the
world a seed and a root of grace and salvation.
This head, which shall be blessed throughout
all generations, is the Word made flesh.　But
God prepared for the Word a pure spot, where
He might unite Himself to human nature ;
this immaculate spot, the virginal spot in the
world of souls, is the Virgin conceived without
sin.

This sinlessness is a privilege of Mary, given
to her *for* all.　God willed to prepare for
the Son of justice a sanctuary in the bosom of
mankind, that the day of light and divine love

might once more arise, after it had been clouded over by darkness and evil.

The Virgin, Queen of mankind, is, after Jesus Christ, the centre and heart of the human race. Mankind, let us never forget, forms but one body, " We are all one body," (Rom. xii. 5.) says St. Paul. This body, thus united, has a heart. And this heart is the soul of Jesus Christ, to which is united the soul of Mary. Mary is essentially the human side in the heart of regenerate mankind ; Jesus is at once the human and the divine. This soul, the centre of the spirit-world, or rather these two souls, which were never soiled by original guilt, became the germ of the new life which was to be infused into the world.

On such a wonderful subject how many things might not be said ! The soul of Jesus and the soul of Mary, two souls in one, form the heart of mankind. If people did but know what a heart is, even the material and visible heart, in the midst of our human body ! The heart is the principle of life ; it gives life to our members, which naturally tend to death. Each separate member, if left to itself, would become exhausted and die. Out of the heart, the principle of life ceases not for an instant to repair this continual decay. By each pulsation it sends life through each member of the body, and also destroys the seeds of death which had there accumulated. Each beat of the heart is twofold, and has two movements ; by one it clears organs of spent blood, by the other it sends forth into them fresh living blood. It is the heart itself which is twofold ;

it is like two hearts in one: the one more active, the other more passive; one which gives life, and the other which removes death to make way for life. The one enlivens, the other purifies.

Such, also, in the centre of regenerate mankind, is the office of its spiritual heart, of this heart composed of two hearts living in one, the soul of Jesus and the soul of Mary. The soul of Jesus gives life to the heart of the world; the soul of Mary, by the grace of Jesus, restores that which was dead to life. She brings back to Him, who is the true Life, the spent blood of mankind, to be restored to life, and to be sent back by Jesus into the world full of life and of grace. The Word, by His incarnation, consecrated our blood, but it is the Virgin who gave Him matter for consecration.

Perhaps another comparison drawn from what passes in the heavens, or among the stars, or in the universe of worlds created by God, will be better understood.

We must know then that all material bodies of whatever form, or however disunited they may be, form one whole, and have one common centre of gravity.* We feel sure that it is a mathematical truth, that there is a centre of gravity in the universe, and that relatively to the whole mass, this centre of gravity is always and necessarily immoveable. The heavens revolve round it with the stars and all the groups of suns. And have we not an

* Salazar, and several other theologians have applied this comparison to the Blessed Virgin.

image of this every night, when we see the polar star itself alone immoveable, in the midst of the others? As therefore, there exists a centre of gravity in the visible universe, a mechanical resting point for the world, immoveable, and which in the midst of all the changes, disturbances and revolutions that have befallen, or shall ever befall, universal matter, preserves an absolute and mathematical immobility—a centre point which a celebrated astronomer has called the throne of God, round which all the stars revolve; so in like manner, there is a point, a centre of gravity in the moral universe, a celestial resting-place for souls, immoveable, and immaculate, in the midst of the agitation and troubles of evil and error. This point is the Incarnate Word; but it is inseparably united to another point, the virginal point in the world of souls, which the Holy Scripture calls "the throne of God," and "the woman crowned with stars," and with it forms a twofold centre.

We may take yet another comparison from the knowledge of the human mind.

Do we believe that the human is entirely fallible, or always, absolutely, and without exception infallible? Certainly neither the one nor the other. Error creeps into our thoughts and our faculties. Nevertheless, St. Thomas of Aquin and Bossuet, not to mention others, teach that our reason is based on an infallible point; failing which our minds would necessarily be unable to arrive at any certainty. If my reason was fallible always, in all things, without exception, nothing would be certain.

I could not be sure of anything, not even of my own existence, nor that of God, nor that of the world, nor of revelation. There would be a positive gulf for ever impassable, fixed between the mind of man and all truth. But there is in reality, a fundamental and central operation of the mind which does not deceive us. "There error enters not," says St. Thomas; and Bossuet exclaims, in his "Elévations sur les Mystères," "O my soul, listen in the depths of thy mind! listen not in the regions of imagination, but listen where the truth makes itself heard, where pure and simple ideas have their abode." This sanctuary, this interior depth, where truth shines clear, is the virginal point of the mind.

In like manner, mankind collectively has its own virginal point: it is the Virgin conceived without sin, or rather it is the Virgin united to the manhood of the Saviour. God reserved for Himself this sanctuary, this immaculate tabernacle in the bosom of fallen mankind. In the midst of our degraded mass, the grace of the Saviour has preserved a leaven of health, to be the divine antidote for our evils. Here is the mystery of Mary, and of her Immaculate Conception. And if this great mystery is as it were an innate idea of our minds, an original impression upon our hearts, as it is on the visible heavens, and on the movements of the stars, does it follow that this mystery is only the necessary result of the nature of things? Far from it. It is, on the contrary, one more proof that God, to whose mind the whole creation is present from all eternity, who conceives at the same moment, the world of nature and the world of grace, and who has only created the first as a means to the second, has seen good to make the first an image and a figure of the second, as the old Testament is the figure of the eternal Testament of the law of grace.

O my God, would that I might never lose sight of these great truths! But how seldom does the smallest ray enter my mind! Yet it is no wonder; my thoughts run on all things except the truth; I spend my time on anything rather than on the study of my religion and its mysteries; I let sleep consume more than a third part of my days; the care of my body claims a great part of my working hours; but who thinks of giving half-an-hour a day to meditate on the truth? When was there in my soul a silence of half-an-hour to listen to God? If in time past I have ever had a taste of this sabbath of the soul, it remains long in my memory as a revelation of a truer life; but why do I never seek to renew the taste? Why do I not let my soul rest in God for one short hour each day? Why do not I strive to gain by prayer the light of truth, whose smallest ray kindles an enduring life in the soul, and enlightens for ever the mind which it pierces? Is it not for want of this inner vision, that I too often understand nothing of the books I read, or of the discourses, the gospels and the truths which the Church sets before me ?

O Mary, thou who art the centre of purity in the world of souls, teach me to direct my soul towards that centre of my understanding and of my will, where the truth makes its voice to be heard. Maintain me in the resolution of neglecting the outside of life, and of exploring its foundation, of interrupting for an hour each day, my habitual intercourse with the outer darkness, to converse in silence with the inner light which God kindles in the centre of the soul, where the mind strikes its roots in the heart, and the heart in God.

MEDITATION VIII.

Queen, conceived without sin, pray for us !

Let us once more, with greater fervour, direct our minds to this mystery of Mary, and of her ever immaculate purity. It is the mystery of mankind, it is one of the roots of the Incarnation, it is one of the threads of the eternal history of mankind, of that providential plan which God designed from all eternity for the salvation of His creatures, and the glorifying of His works.

Let us read and meditate that which the great St. Francis of Sales wrote about the plan of God's supernatural Providence.

" Every thing which God has done, is de-

signed for the salvation of men and of angels;
by attention to the Holy Scriptures, and to
the doctrine of the Fathers, we shall see that
this is the order of Providence, so far as our
weakness allows us to utter it.

" From all eternity, God considered that
He was able to create an innumerable quantity
of creatures of different perfections and quali-
ties, to whom He might communicate Himself; and seeing that among all the ways of
communicating Himself, there was none so
excellent, as that of uniting Himself to some
created nature, so that the creature should be
as it were morticed and grafted into the Godhead, so as to form with It one sole person,
His infinite goodness, which is naturally in-
clined to communicate itself, resolved and
determined to make a communication of this
kind, in order that, as from all eternity there
is an essential communication in God, by
which the Father communicates His whole and
indivisible Godhead to the Son in begetting
Him, and the Father and the Son together
in the procession of the Holy Ghost, communicate to Him also the unity of their own
Godhead; in the same way this sovereign
Mercy should be also so perfectly communi-
cated to a creature, that the created nature
and the Godhead each preserving their own
properties, should nevertheless be · so united
together, as to be but one person."...

" Thus, after the Providence of God had
made from all eternity the project and design
of all that He was to create, He willed and loved
with a preference regulated by the order of

excellence, first of all the most excellent object
of His love, that is, our Saviour, and next in
their order, the other creatures, according as
they more or less subserve the honour and
glory of this same Saviour.

" Thus everything was created for this God-
man, who on this account is called the first-
born of every creature, whom the Lord possessed in the beginning of His ways, before He
had made any single thing, created in the
beginning before the ages ; for in Him all
things were made, and all things are established in Him, and He is the head of the
whole Church, having in all things, and everywhere the primacy. And as in the vine which
we plant principally for its fruit, this fruit is
the first thing in our desire and intention,
although the leaves and the blossoms are
before it in the order of nature ; so the Saviour
was the first in God's intention, and in that
eternal plan which Providence made for His
creation, and it was with a view to this de-
sired fruit that the vine of the universe was
planted, and the course of generation was
established, which, like leaves and blossoms,
were to go before as precursors and fitting
preparatives for the production of that grape
which the Spouse praises in the Canticles, and
whose juice cheereth both God and men.

" God had so mixed up the appetites of
His creatures with their will, that the appetite
forced not the will, but left it its liberty ; and
He foresaw that a part, the smaller part of the
angels would voluntarily renounce His holy
love, and would in consequence lose their

glory. But there was this difference between the nature of angels and that of men, that the angels could only sin by express malice, without any temptation or motive which could excuse them; whereas man was feeble by nature, a breath that passes and comes not again, subject to be surprised by temptation.''*

This is why the fall of the Angels was irreparable; but that of man, though irreparable by himself, was redeemed by the infinite mercy and love of God.

Let us try to understand the mystery of the fall, and of the redemption.

We sometimes hear it said, Why did God create the world, if He foresaw that His work would be overcome by evil, and that the largest part of His creation would fall for ever under its yoke?

But where do we see that the work of God has been overcome by evil?

The work of God, as it existed in His idea from all eternity, is principally the God-man, for whose sake all the rest was made, who is the crowning fruit of the creation, and in comparison with whom, all the rest is nothing, since He is of infinite worth. Now this God-man was never overcome by evil, but overcame it.

Next to the God-man in the work of the creation, stands His Mother, who by herself surpasses in excellence and worth, all other creatures; the Mother of God was never overcome by evil, or tainted by it, in any sense whatever.

* Traité de l' Amour de Dieu, book 2, chap. v. and vi.

The third place in God's work is occupied
by that great and overwhelming majority of
the angels, who rejected the evil, and freely
chose the good.

In the fourth place, we find those immense multitudes of souls which lived only
a few hours or a few days upon earth, and
never actually sinned, but were only deprived
by Adam's sin, of the holy state of original
grace to which the Saviour has restored them.

In the next place come those other legions
of souls, which have sinned actually, but which
the Redeemer has saved by the greater abundance of His grace.

Now in order to create these numberless
companies of souls and spirits, able to chose
the good part of the love of God, as God had
chosen them, it was necessary to create them
free. Hence it was also necessary to admit
the possibility of several of these spirits and
souls refusing to love God. But this free re-
jection of God makes their worth incomparably
less than that of the least of glorified spirits,
and we might almost say that all of them
together are become so insignificant through
their approach to nothingness, that they *are*
nothing in comparison to the least of the elect.

Where, then, do we find that God's work
has been overcome by evil?

That part of creation which did not remain
in the Love of God is, in comparison to the
City of God, but a wreath of smoke and a vain
and empty shadow. The other part is the
great body of creatures predestined to eternal
love.

This is the mystery of the fall. But the mystery of redemption requires a new illustration. We must know her who co-operated with the work, our Queen conceived without sin, as well as the cause, the author, and the principle of the work, who is God Himself our King.

"God," continues St. Francis of Sales, "prepared for His most holy Mother a favour worthy of the love of a Son, who being all-wise, all-mighty, and all-good, could prepare Himself a Mother after His own heart. He willed, then, that His redemption should be applied to her in the way of a preservative, so that the sin which descended from generation to generation should not touch her, and that His sacred Mother, like a thing set apart for her Son, should be redeemed by Him not only from damnation but from all danger of damnation, and should be assured of all grace in all its perfection, and should thus come forth like a beautiful morning, which having once begun its dawn continually increases its brightness even to perfect day. Wonderful redemption, masterpiece of the Redeemer, first of all redemptions, whereby the Son, in the true filial tenderness of His heart, forestalled His Mother with the blessings of His mercy, and preserved her not only from sin like the angels, but also from all danger of sin, and from all the difficulties and hindrances to the exercise of holy love. And thus He protests that among all the reasonable creatures whom He has chosen, His Mother is His dove, His only one, His all-perfect and all-cherished one, best beloved beyond all proportion or comparison."*

This, then, was the eternal plan of the world.

The Sun of justice, truth, and holiness, enlightens all things, vivifies all with His divine light. This Sun is the incarnate Word, the splendour of eternal light, the Man-God; but it is also the Mother of the Word, who is perfectly united to Him, who is in Him as He is in her, who clothes Him as she is clothed by Him, who bears Him in her womb, and at the same time is encompassed, enfolded, and encircled by Him, for she is truly "that woman clothed with the sun," of which Holy Scripture speaks; therein dwell two human hearts united in everlasting purity, that of Christ and that of His holy Mother. This is the centre, the immutable foundation of the work of God. Round this heart of the world revolve millions of other hearts and souls united to it, which in spite of many trials and fallings away, return again and again to their allegiance; and after long wanderings in exile, and frequent vicissitudes of fortune, have once more regained their centre, the source of true light and true love, and the place of eternal repose; who either by love, by free choice, by sufferings, or by labours and combats, have won back their inheritance, and have found how the Father of the world, together with the Mother of the Word and of mankind, is the brother, the friend, the husband of souls, the perfect

* Traité de l'Amour de Dieu, II. 6.

model and principle of all love, of all strength, and of the courage which is needed for those labours and sufferings which lead men to heaven. This is the work of God.

And beyond the immense sphere of light which forms the aureole of the sun, its rays drive away and dissipate like smoke or shadows those contemptible and guilty souls, who are without love and full of darkness, and who have chosen to remain isolated and opposed to all, and outside of God.

O my God, I will henceforth have greater faith in the reality of this central sun of the justice and truth, of the life and love of heaven, and also in the reality of the outer darkness of hell. I shall understand that like those wandering stars of which St. James speaks, I gravitate towards heaven, but that I may, like them, be carried out of my sphere of attraction by my heaviness, or by some false impulse, and be lost in the fathomless abyss. I see that the life of my soul is ever at war with these two contrary forces, which are known to all men by their effects, but of whose cause they are for the most part ignorant. These two forces must ever be acting upon us. Can heaven do otherwise than attract me? Here is one force. Can my own inertia, hurried along in the vortex of time, do otherwise than carry me away from heaven? Here is the second force. Can those spirits of light and of peace, who watch my conflict, do otherwise than draw me by their prayers and their love? And can the contagious example of the wicked,

the spirit of unbelief, rebellion, and schism,
the spirit of pride, self-love and sensuality,
fail to allure me, unless I have overcome them
and ejected them from my heart by my free-
will? Now I know the meaning of these two
attractions, and I shall be able to distinguish
their contrary movements within my soul, and
to put in the scale of heaven the weight of my
love, for as St. Augustine says, " My love is
the weight which measures my worth."

———

MEDITATION IX.

Mother most pure, pray for us.

Let us never be weary of endeavouring by
prayer and meditation, by desire for light, and
by thankfulness for its least ray, to go deeper
and deeper into the thought of the mystery
of Mary's Immaculate purity. This mystery
is in some sort the vital centre of God's work,
as well as its governing force, and the sure
hope of those who are wrestling, and are still
journeying on.

If we wish for further enlightenment on
this subject, let us seek it in the sublime teaching of St. Augustine.

" Thou, O Lord, hast taught me, by Thine
All-powerful voice, speaking in the interior
of my soul, that Thou alone art eternal, and
immortal, that there is nothing variable in
Thee; that Thy will subsisted in its immuta-

bility before time was; for a will subject to change would cease to be an immortal will. I see these things in the light of Thy presence, O Lord; but I pray Thee, grant me an increase of this light, and that under the influence of this revelation I may dwell beneath Thy wings in humility and littleness.

"Thou hast again taught me, O my God, by Thine All-powerful word, speaking in the midst of my soul, that all nature, and everything that is not Thyself, was made by Thee. That alone which is not, as well as every action of will which turns aside from Thee, who art, to that which is less, is not Thy work; for these acts are evil and sin. Moreover, no sin can affect Thee, O Lord, nor can in any way disturb the order of Thy will. This, O Lord, is what Thou hast revealed to me in the light of Thy presence, and I pray Thee to grant me an increase of this light, that through this revelation I may for ever dwell beneath Thy wings in humility and littleness.

"Still further hast Thou told me, by Thine All-powerful voice, speaking in the ear of my soul, of a created being, who, though she has no will but Thine, is not co-eternal with Thee; who by her constant chastity lived for Thee alone; and who, though she was capable of change, remained steadfast; she fixed her whole love on Thee, O Lord, who art ever present, and therefore had no doubt for the future, no remorse for the past, no vicissitudes to undergo, and no changes of season to experience. O ever blessed is that soul by her

firm adherence to Thy beatitude, ever blessed
by the eternal and intimate hospitality which
she gives to Thee, and by the eternal brightness which she receives! And what shall
I call the heaven of heavens, which is
God's, except it be Thy dwelling, O my
God, which contemplates Thee, which is
blessed in Thy blessedness, without falling
away from, or departing from Thee; a spirit
all pure, and perfectly in union with Thee,
who art the everlasting peace of the heavenly
spirits and citizens of the city on high, far
above this visible heaven.

"Let the soul, then, which finds the
way of this pilgrimage too long, understand these things; if even now she thirsts
after Thee, if her tears are become her drink,
if day by day she hears within herself the
question, Where is now thy God? if even now
she seeks and desires but one thing, that she
may dwell for ever in Thy house. O my God,
let her, if she can, understand what eternity
is in comparison with time, because even now
Thy holy house, which has ever been with
Thee, although it is not co-eternal with Thee,
experiences no change of time, because it remains united to Thee, without inconstancy or
change. This, O God, is what I see in the
light of Thy presence, and grant that this light
may increase, and that through this revelation
I may for ever dwell beneath Thy wings in
humility and littleness."

Thus speaks the great St. Augustine; and
after this description of the most holy of creatures, perfect in the contemplation of God,

which has never fallen away, and which nothing has ever separated from God, he adds :

" Will you call that error which the truth teaches me, by God's All-powerful word, speaking to the ear of my soul ; what is there here for contradiction to contradict ?

" Will you deny that there is such a perfect creature, continually united to the eternal and the true God, by so chaste a love, that without being co-eternal with Him, yet being never distracted from Him, she knows not time nor its changes, but ever remains in the repose of eternal contemplation ? Thou dost manifest Thyself to her, O Lord, and it sufficeth her, and never do her desires tend towards herself, or towards aught but Thee. This is the house of God, a house not made of earth, nor even of the matter of the heavens ; but spiritual, and partaking of Thy eternity, because it is eternally without spot. Thou hast founded her for ever ; it is a law which Thou hast made, and which shall not be broken. Yet this divine dwelling is not eternal, for it had a beginning, it was created.

" Not that we can find any time before her, for wisdom was created before all things—not the Wisdom which is equal and co-eternal with God His Father, and our God, by whom all things were made, the Lord of heaven and earth ; but that other created wisdom, the intellectual nature, which is light through the contemplation of the Light, and which, though created, is also called wisdom. As the Light that illumines differs from the light that is illu-

3

mined, so does the Wisdom that creates differ
from created wisdom; so does essential Justice
differ from our imparted justice.   There is,
then, a wisdom anterior to all created things,
itself created; it is the intelligent and reasonable soul of Thy holy city, our heavenly
Mother, which is free, and lives in heaven for
ever ; in that heaven of heavens which praises
Thee, herself being the heaven of heavens,
which is the Lord's; and although we find no
time before her, because she precedes the
creation of time, yet before this wisdom there
is the eternity of God who created her, and
who gave her her beginning."

Let us meditate carefully on this prayer,
dedicated by the light of wisdom, and whose
depth of doctrine has perhaps never been sufficiently commented on.

And first we should notice that the illus-
trious Father of the Church, who is the chief
authority in the West, here declares with a
strength of affirmation which is seldom met with
throughout his writings, that this doctrine was
revealed· to him by the Holy Spirit, with the
clearness, and with the almighty power of a
voice speaking to his soul.

And what does he teach?   He teaches that
there is one sublime created being, who is our
heavenly Mother, in whom God dwells, and
who from the first hour of her creation lived
without any change, or the least falling away,
but always and entirely united to God.

But who is this sublime creature?   According to St. Augustine, it is she of whom Holy
Scripture speaks: " The Lord possessed me

in the beginning of His ways, before He made any thing from the beginning ;" and elsewhere, " Wisdom was created before all things."

Now, to whom does the Catholic Church apply these words of Holy Scripture ? To the Virgin, Mother of God, and to the human nature of Jesus Christ. These well-known texts constantly occur in the office of the Blessed Virgin.*

No doubt the holy doctor applies all he says here about created wisdom, to the world of angels; for this heavenly society really is a creation which, from the very beginning, was faithful in the contemplation of God, without falling away, or change. But there is something above the angels ; there is the Queen of angels, there is the human nature of the Saviour. In the intention of God and in His divine plan, there existed before and above the angels the two crowning works of the creation, the human nature of Jesus Christ and the Blessed Virgin, the Mother of Jesus. The fore-ordained design of the Incarnation, which implies the sublime vocation of Mary, is, as S. Francis of Sales explains it, the principle and the cause of the creation, and the beginning of the ways of God. If, then, there is a first and chief creation, which S. Augustine calls created wisdom, and which ever remains un-failingly united to God, so that nothing was

---

* And therefore the very words which Holy Scripture uses of the uncreated Wisdom, and of His eternal generation, the Church uses both in her offices and in her liturgy, in reference to the Conception of the Blessed Virgin, which was determined in one and the same decree with the Incarnation of the divine Wisdom. (Apostolic letters of Pius IX., touching the definition of the dog-ma of the Immaculate Conception.)

ever able to separate it from Him for a single
instant, how can it be said that the Mother of
the Word, who was destined from all eternity
to be the Queen of this holy creation, in the
same way as the Incarnate Word was to be
its head and its king—how can it be said that
the Mother of the Word Incarnate was ever,
for a single instant, subject to the powers of
darkness and separated from God, while the
angels, her servants, persevered in their unchanging contemplation, and in their unfailing
union with God?*

O Mary, who didst give to the Word His
body, and thereby didst shed eternal light over
the world, pray for us, that the light of these
profound mysteries, which now glimmers upon
us from afar, may shine more brightly before
us, and that in this light we may for ever
dwell beneath the wings of God, and under
thy wings, O Mother of souls, in child-like
humility and littleness! My desire, O Lord,
is to enter into this light. I desire, like St.
Augustine, to feel how I am an exile, to know
what eternity is with regard to time, and to
labour to liken to eternity the time which is
given me. Eternal life in its fulness is the
contemplation, the possession of light and love,
without the possibility of change. Time, like
the succession of which we are conscious, is
the succession and change from night to day.
My soul, in its present state, sees the light by
fits and starts. The day of the soul, according

* "Always conversing with God, and joined with Him in
an everlasting covenant, she was never in darkness, but always
in light." (Apostolic letters of Pius IX.)

to the masters of the spiritual life, is a ray
which shines by intervals. The soul which
has had a glimpse of the light knows this well.
She knows how soon the light grew pale, and
then went out; and how when she sought it
again, it was nowhere to be found. She had
experienced a moment of life and joy and fervour; she thought it would continue on for
ever; but time went on, its changeful wheel
went round, and the sun buried all his warmth
and light beneath the horizon. Regret and
remembrance alone remain. Regret, for not
having profited by the day. "Whilst you
have the light, believe in the light," says the
Saviour, "that you may become children of the
light." This is what I now intend to put in
practice, that the time Thou givest me may be
the beginning of eternity. When the ray
returns, I will believe in it more firmly; I
shall know that it is not my light, O my God,
but Thine; I shall know that the light will
soon be darkened; I will not delay, but will
at once submit myself to Thee, O Light of my
soul, that I may become a child of light,
according to Thy promise. Then the ray will
not depart so quickly, the night will not come
so soon. The days of my soul will grow
longer, as when the sun approaches its sum-
mer solstice. The daylight of my mind and
my heart will be only interrupted by short
nights, and perhaps before I enter into the
full daylight of eternity, I also, like the saints,
shall enjoy one of those long polar days which
are such vivid types of eternity; nightless
days, when the sun only stoops towards the

horizon and touches it, to show when it should
be midnight, but not to set behind it.

———

MEDITATION X.

Mother Immaculate, pray for us.

To throw light on the great mystery of human
salvation, which comprises the victory over
sin, the redemption of souls, and the channel of
Redemption, let us now have recourse to an
authority yet higher than St. Augustine. Let
us open the Holy Scriptures.

We will not take isolated texts, and bring
them together from all parts of the Bible, but
we will read through whole chapters. Neither
will we choose these chapters according to our
own fancy; but we will take those which the
Catholic Church has selected for the office of
the Blessed Virgin. Let us listen with rever-
ence to these words of pure inspiration, which
are, as it were, the mystical incarnation of
Christ. And let us not forget that this created wisdom, whose praises we are reading, is
the principle, the heart, the centre of all creation, and is the type, first of the human nature
of the Saviour, and then of the Mother of
God.

" Wisdom bears in herself her own glory,
which comes from God, and which shines forth
before men.

" She shall open her mouth in the assembly
of saints, and shed abroad the Light of God.

"In the midst of souls God exalts her and glorifies her in the fulness of holiness.

"Among the multitude of the elect, her glory is seen. She is blessed among the blessed, and she says:

"I am the first-born of creatures, I came forth before all from the mouth of God.

"By me that light arose in the heavens, which shall never fail, and like a fertile cloud I covered the earth.

"My dwelling is in the centre of the universe, and my throne is the pivot of the worlds.

"I alone am above the heavens; I alone have penetrated into the deep; I have walked through the oceans of creation, and all its worlds, and in every nation, in every assembly of free beings, I am the Queen.

"By my power I am exalted above the most noble hearts, and I am more lowly than the humblest. In all this I do but seek repose in God, and peace in His inheritance.

"But the Creator of all things made known to me His Will. He that made me willed also to dwell in me, as in a tabernacle, and He said to me: Dwell among my people, share the heritage of those who are mine, and take root in the souls of my elect.

"I was created in the beginning and before all ages; I live in the age to come, and I minister to God in His holy dwelling-place.

"I am strength in holy souls, repose in the holy city, and in Jerusalem I am Queen.

"I am the Queen of those chosen souls who

inherit the portion of God, my abode is in the full assembly of saints.

" I am the cedar of Lebanon, and the cypress of the Mountain of Sion; the palm-tree of Cades, and the rose-tree of Jericho; the rich olive-tree of the plain, and the plane-tree by the water's side. I am like an aromatic balm, and the choicest myrrh; the purest perfumes are found in me.

" I stretch out my boughs like the turpentine-tree, and my branches are of honour and grace.

"I am the fruitful vine, I am its perfume and its fruit.

" I am the mother of pure love, of filial fear, and of holy hope.

" In me is that grace which is the way and the truth.; in me is the hope of life and virtue.

" Come to me, you who love me, and feed yourselves with my fruit.

" My spirit is sweetness itself, my inheritance is sweeter than honey.

" Time brings no forgetfulness to my memory.

" He that feeds on me shall yet hunger, and he that drinks of me shall yet thirst.

" He that harkeneth to me shall never be confounded, and he that works with me shall never sin.

" He that brings me to light, has eternal life.

" All this is the book of life, the covenant of the Most High, and the manifestation of truth.

" Moses gave the precepts of the law; he gave to Jacob an inheritance, and promises to Israel; but to David, his elect, was it given to beget the mighty King, who should sit upon the eternal throne.

" This is He who gives abundance of Wisdom, like the overflowing courses of the Tigris and the Phison.

" This is He who gives increase to the understanding, as Euphrates increaseth its waters at the time of harvest.

" This is He who pours forth light and truth, as Gehon pours abroad its waters at the time of the vintage.

" He alone knows her in perfection; another weaker than He shall never know her entirely.

" He is more than a river of wisdom, and more than an abyss of light.

" I, wisdom, pour out the rivers which come from Him.

" I am the bed of the river, its source, its spring, the channel, by which it flows out of Paradise.

" I have but to say: I will water my gardens, my meadows; I will inundate them with fatness; and immediately the waters flow and the river becomes like a sea.

" Yes, I am the dawn which brings light to all, and before long I spread it afar.

" I dive down into the lowest parts of the earth, I awaken those that sleep, and enlighten all who hope in God." (Eccle. xxiv.)*

* Although this translation seems to us exact, yet it cannot claim in any way the authority of the text approved by the

In this passage of Scripture we find the
channel of graces, the dawn which is the pre-
cursor of the sun, the gate of heaven, the
source and spring of the river which fertilizes
the earth, the humility and purity which
stimulate the hunger and thirst after justice
and truth. Here we see the Mother of fair
love and of holy hope, who is the depository of grace, of whom He was born, who is
the way, the truth, and the life. We see
here the Queen of the holy city, the fellow-
worker with God, the minister of His power; we
see her who though God's creature, yet brought
into the world the eternal Light, and we find
innumerable other mysteries, the consideration
of which would take up many days.

And the Holy Spirit tells us that this wisdom shall endure throughout future ages, and
that she shall contemplate the face of God in
His heavenly dwelling-place for ever.

The following is the other portion of the
sacred text, which the Catholic Church uses
in the offices of the Nativity and the Conception of the Blessed Virgin.

" God possessed me in the beginning of His
ways, before He brought forth any germ of
creation.

" I was predestined and ordained from all
eternity, and I stood in the presence of God
before the earth was made.

" The depths were not as yet, and I was
already conceived, nor had the fountains yet
sprung out. I was born before the moun-

Church. It should be compared with the text, but should be
looked upon, at least in certain places, only as a paraphrase.

tains or the hills were set up; before the
formation of the world and the first impulse of
its movement I was begotten by God.

" When God prepared the heavens I was
present with Him; when He gave to matter
its laws and its movement; when He launched
forth the stars into space, and poised their yet
fluid masses; when He gave the sea its limits,
and the law which hinders it from passing its
bounds; when He gave the globe of the earth
its centre of gravity, I was with God, co-
operating in all His works, full of joy in those
first days of the world, always before His face,
playing with delight in the midst of the new-
created world, and above all in the souls of
men." (Prov. viii. 22.)

O my God, it is then true that Thou hast
spoken to the earth sacred words which reveal
the secrets of heaven. Thou hast given holy
books, inspired by Thine own Spirit, which
contain truths whose meaning is unravelled by
degrees; as the world advances and the Church
goes on increasing. How is it that these
books have been so little read and meditated
on by me? Why have I not the inclination,
the intelligence, and the curiosity to study
them? I am too far removed from them in
my heart and in my life. I have not within
me a spark of that internal light without which
I cannot comprehend the meaning of the
divine words which sound on my ear. When
I pass from the shallow clearness of common
thoughts to the sacred text, all is dark. But
to the contemplative soul this night will have

its stars, and when she raises her thoughts to heaven, she will see that these stars are worlds, or rather suns and centres of systems. O Lord, I will behold Thy heaven and Thy stars! says the Prophet. I will say the same. I hope also one day, by means of prayer, to attain this state of contemplation, this height whence the soul begins to see heaven, and to discover its mysteries beneath the letter of holy writ.

O Mary, conceived without sin, who wert not only filled with wisdom, but wert in some sort wisdom itself—that created wisdom, in whose praise the Holy Scriptures employ all the wealth of deepest poetry,—unfold to the Christians of this our age the meaning of the Scriptures, that they may see thee therein; and if the Scriptures are truly, as St. Augustine says, a kind of incarnation of Christ, let them learn to contemplate the Mother of Christ as present where Christ is, in the same way as on the altar we recognize the blood of Jesus Christ which was derived from that of the Virgin, the Mother of regenerated man.

MEDITATION XI.

Queen, clothed with the sun, pray for us!

Let us meditate on this glorious and wonderful title which the beloved disciple was inspired by God to give to the Blessed Virgin, who was made his Mother by the word of the Saviour on the cross.

St. John, in the vision of Patmos, exclaims:
" A great sign appeared in heaven : a woman
clothed with the sun, and the moon under her
feet, and on her head a crown of twelve stars,
bearing a child in her womb. . . . . a man-child,
who was to rule all nations." (Apoc. xii.)

The woman who brings forth the King of
nations is the Virgin. She then must also be
the woman clothed with the sun. But what
is this sun if it be not the Sun of justice, the
Word of God?

St. John's wonderful words show us the
invisible world of souls under the image of the
visible world of the stars. And it would be
impossible to have any symbol at once so
beautiful and so true.

The stars are grouped in clusters and act
on each other with forces which bind them
together in indissoluble unity. So it is with
souls; all are rooted in God, each attracts the
rest, all support each other.

But these planetary stars have a common
centre, from which they are all produced.
God brought them forth, each in its time,
from their common source. So it is with
souls in the order of grace. There is a primitive pair, from whom all descend ; the sacred
pair, divine and human—the Father and the
Mother of souls.

These stars, moreover, revolve round their
motionless centre, and all receive from its life
light and heat. So it is with souls. They all
revolve round the centre which supports them,.
and thence they derive life, light, and heat.

The centre of these stars is itself a globe, of

the same matter and the same nature as the rest, only this central world is clothed with light, while the other worlds are not.

So is it with souls. There is but one which is clothed with the sun. The others live in the exterior light of the sun, beyond the aureole, of which she alone occupies the inner-most centre.

And in this symbol I read the whole history of souls. No one has yet found a suitable comparison between the state of souls in their journey through time, and the state of their earthly habitations. The orbs which whirl round the sun give a wonderfully accurate notion of the state of our souls in this life.

Enter into your soul and view it in this light. What do you see?

I see, first of all, that my soul is always active, never at rest; she is ever tending and aspiring to something she has not; she tends and aspires to some better state, to some higher life. My soul is ever in motion, wan-dering and planetary like the earth which car-ries me. My soul is ever looking forward to the morrow, and hurrying over her days in hopes of finding a better.

The earth, which travels so fast, moves not faster than my soul. Of these two planets my soul is the more active; she it is who would often hasten the speed of the vessel, and who cries out with the Prophet, either by desire or by prayer: Lord, shorten the time, hasten the end.

But is my soul, though ever desiring better things, always advancing in goodness? Does she march straight towards her life, her light, her happiness, towards justice and truth? No, if I have any quality at all, it is changeableness. The softest and the brightest flashes of light are followed by the most painful darkness, the deepest gloom. Thus my soul passes from day to night, and from night to day, like the earth; the more my mind labours to approach the truth the more clearly it sees that the day turns naturally to night, and the night to day. I witness the dawn in my soul, I see the dawn brightening into day; a day sometimes clear, sometimes cloudy; but as sure as noon-day comes I see the light, always uncertain, begin to wane, to darken into twilight and vanish into night. But neither in the earth, nor in my soul, is the movement useless that carries us over from day to day. For through all these alternations of light and darkness, unless my soul transgresses her law by abusing her liberty, she sees her days lengthen and her nights shorten, as she advances in light. She perceives that the progress is real, and that the movement tends to something. The gifts of life develop within me first the flower then the fruit, beginning with the least, going on to the more precious, and ending with the two great supports of my life. But already, whilst these fruits are ripening, the days have begun to shorten; my soul no longer enjoys the same fulness of light, the same abundance of sap, the same warmth, the same glory. She sees with grief that her life is waning, in spite of all her efforts; she feels that her end is approaching, and that death must come. Then she droops her branches, she retires little by little into herself; and as in a plant that lives but a year, all that is seen dies down while its life concentrates itself in the roots under ground, till spring comes again; so shall my soul quit the visible world, she shall leave her body and all her earthly trappings, and shall concentrate herself in God, her indestructible root; till the Father summons her again to life. Thus my soul, like the earth or the planets, has her days and her years, and the world is a book wherein I read the phases of her life.

Still this is but a feeble comparison; for the earth and its productions are only symbols for our instruction, they are figures which write what God dictates, and obey Him in all things. The soul, on the contrary, is free. By the abuse of her liberty, the soul may change this order. At times she shortens days that God would lengthen; she prevents the gathering in of the harvest, though God sows the seed and sends His sun to ripen the fruit. Sometimes even she closes her life with refusing to return to God.

The soul is capable of sinning: she does sin—we see it every day. She lives or dies, she waxes or wanes according to her free choice. She undergoes also, in her moral life, an alternation too little understood; an alternation of strength and weakness in her combat with evil; of strength which God gives, of weakness which He permits; a strength and weakness, given and permitted to teach us to conquer and to grow in strength. Yes, each soul during the journey of this life bears within her both

weakness and strength, both virtue and sin.
There are seeds of virtue, principles of an eternal law, which the Word by His continual
presence preserves within us; and there is
original sin, which by its nature inclines always
to actual sin, and which man by the help of
God is bound to overcome.

Faith teaches us, and reason and experience
prove that no man can, by himself, conquer
sin, nor advance in the knowledge and practice
of virtue, nor bear fruits of justice for the life
to come. Without the help of God, there
would be neither lengthening of the day nor
season of fruitfulness, neither flowers, nor
fruit. Left to himself man would continually
wane, and would bring gradual decay on all
he touched; the first occasion of temptation
and estrangement from God would necessitate
a fall, and man would be precipitated through
the darkness to the chill embrace of death, like
a star shot out from its orbit, and no longer
revolving round its centre.

But God has constituted a moral world in
which life is possible, and in which life must
triumph for all men who do not absolutely reject it.

He has placed, in the midst of the multitudinous assembly of souls, a centre of life, of
light and of strength, as in the midst of the
universe He has placed the sun.

The visible sun is not that universal æther
which percolates and pervades every atom of
each world, and which is the principle of all
light, of all movement, and of all force, an invisible fluid that supports, envelops, and pene-

trates all visible things; but the centres of systems, the suns which we see, are incarnations of this fluid, attached to an orb of the same substance and nature as the planetary bodies, which in themselves are dark and opaque.

Yes, there is a mass of common matter, an earth like ours, in the centre of each system, and with it are bound up all the active and sensible forces of the universal æther. This central mass is enveloped with an immense atmosphere of light and heat. And this solar atmosphere is the source of light. It is the source of the force which supports the planets, which moves them, illuminates them, and warms them; it is the centre which attracts them all towards itself, and prevents their motion degenerating into an endless tumble through space. It rolls each planet on its axis, and causes the alternations of day and night, and the annual succession of the seasons.

This is an image of the sun of souls, which is not only the eternal and creator Spirit, such as He is in Himself.—It is not simply the great God, everywhere present, and pervading all beings with His own essence.—It is not the pure absolute infinite Being who is invisible to us.—It is the same God, undoubtedly, but in His new form, as incarnate in our nature, and in a being like ourselves. Here is the source which supplies all the wants of our souls; here is the centre, the force which holds and bears them up, which enlightens, warms, and vivifies them. It is

He who never ceases to attract them lest their
motion should become an eternal fall; it is He
who renews the light of each soul, after it has
been buried in darkness; it is He who allows
temptation to endure but for a season, and
then causes it to give place to light and
strength.   But the true sun, the Incarnate
God, who is at once both earth and æther,
matter and force, two elements radically distinct, but perfectly combined in the unity of
light, this Sun, I say, is not in solitude at the
centre of the world. As the inspired word of
St. John assures us, He has clothed with His
radiance the woman from whom He sprang.
And in the same way as beneath the shining
light which is properly the sun, astronomers
see at times a kernel, a globe, an earth,
which by itself would be dark and opaque
like our earth; so also, but much more
surely, the true centre of the world of souls,
is the great sign of which St. John speaks,
" *the woman clothed with the sun,*" with the
great light who is her Son, who is her God.
So that the divine Sun of Justice, who became
incarnate on this earth, was not content with
merely deriving from this central earth the
substance which He united to His divinity;
it pleased Him also that this chosen earth,
by a singular privilege, should continue in
Him, should remain there immoveable like
Himself, in the midst of the planetary globes;
it pleased Him that she should be there without alternation, in the midst of worlds ever
alternating; He would not suffer that this
chosen earth, the Mother of the Day, should

ever have been shrouded in night. It pleased
Him that she should always have dwelled and
ever should dwell in the light, and should be
clothed with it in all ways through all time.
It pleased Him to keep her altogether immaculate.

Thus, if it is a question, why the central
earth is not planetary, like other globes, we
say that, by her very centrality, she must
necessarily be in repose, while all the rest,
being at a distance from the centre, have no
choice but to revolve round the circumference.

If you would know why this earth alone
was never buried in night, we say, as she
provided the sun with the fuel from which his
flames shine forth, she is necessarily girt round
and absorbed in his radiance. The night
which all other orbs must feel, because
they are opaque and at a distance from the
sun, is impossible for her, who though dark in
herself like the others, is preserved from all
the shades of night, by the flame which she
feeds, and which clothes her with the day as
with a garment.

This is the woman clothed with the sun;
this is the one chosen soul whose garment is
the sun of justice. How could the night of
sin ever have darkened around her? It may
darken around all other souls, she alone is
excepted. Why should there be this exception? Because it is in the constitution of
the world. The world of souls is a living
system; and in every system the central body
stands alone, apart from all the rest. The
central point remains immoveable while all

the rest revolve around it. When, as in our
solar system, the central body is surrounded
with a luminous atmosphere, that body alone
is within the atmosphere, all the rest are
without; it alone has the atmosphere all round
it, all points of its surface are in the light;
the other orbs are only illuminated on one
side, while the other is plunged in darkness
and shadow.

But why was the world made on this plan?
Why should there be a centre? Why has the
centre these prerogatives? Why do life, force,
and light, come from it? I cannot tell *why*
it is so, but I see *that* it is; when the question
is about the material world I see with my
eyes; when the question is about the spiritual
world, why should I not believe? Perhaps
this plan makes the world of souls the most
exact image of God. In any case, is not this
the only arrangement that can reduce all to
unity? The centre is the unity in which all
ought to live; the prerogatives of this centre
are the treasures of all. Is not this arrangement also the only one which could make the
world a school for educating the freedom of
created spirits?

My God, in all this beautiful imagery which
my mind has been dwelling on, is there not more
to be found than a mere temporary food for
the mystical soul who seeks in all things the
image of what she loves? Is it not true that
in the whole of Thy work, as in a book may
be read the mysteries of eternity? Thou
createst and governest all conformably to
Thyself, O Lord; Thy eternal plan is the

image of Thyself. Thy consubstantial image,. Thy Word Incarnate in Thy work is the end of Thy work, it is its principle, its reason, and its cause, as it is also its consummation. But after Him the principal part of Thy work is that created being who, from all eternity, was destined by Thy wisdom to give a body to the Incarnate Word, to conceive the Eternal Word, and to spread It abroad in ever-increasing abundance over that which did not as yet exist. Behold, O Lord, this is Thy Sun, a union of the Incarnate Word, and of the Mother who conceived the Word. Around this Sun Thou hast planted in Thy love other souls, that is, other centres of love, that they may drink in its light, and become like to it. These are the stars gifted with intelligence and free-will, which surround Thy Sun, and which crown the woman clothed with the Sun. When Thou hadst thus designed the world of souls, it pleased Thee to make the world of bodies in like sort, and Thou didst create it as we see it, because all things are created by Thee conformably to Thyself, and according to Thy eternal plan, which is no other than Thine own image.

The only thing, O Lord, which Thy visible world does not teach us, is how these planetary souls can come to their eternal and unchangeable perfection, or how souls illuminated by an outward light, can become self-luminous, and the centres of an atmosphere of light. This is only taught us by Thy Gospel.

But whatever may be the uncertainty and the weakness of our suppositions, O Lord, one thing is true, that my soul is a pilgrim, and that she takes repose. She has only a partial light, which comes but at intervals, while she seeks a light which is full and enduring. Thus it is with all men.

Therefore is it good for us to know the laws and the source of light, " by what way the light is spread," * that we may come to it, and bear its fruits.

———

MEDITATION XII.

Queen of Ages, pray for us.

If Thou art the King of Ages, O Lord Jesus, Thy Mother is the Queen of Ages, for she is by Thy grace, for ever and in all things, all that Thou art by nature and by right.

Do thou, then, O Queen of Ages, pray for us! Pray for the age in which we live, when the Church has raised thine entire and immaculate purity to the dignity of a dogma of faith.

But what is this age in which we live? And what must we ask for it?

An age has always a two-fold character. In every age there are two ages: a holy age, and an evil age. The age as it is given by God, and the age such as it is made by man. There is the spirit and the idea with which God inspires each epoch, and there is the perversion

* Job xxxviii. 24.

which the wicked, the obstinate and the blind
introduce into this divine idea. The evil age
is that of which it is said: "To corrupt and
to be corrupted is the spirit of the age;" and
the good age is that which the prophet speaks
of in these words: "Grant us, O Lord, to
know Thy way upon earth, and Thy salutary
dealings with all people." The knowledge of
the ways of God in every epoch and in every
nation, is the spirit of the good age. What
then is the characteristic of the evil age?

As evil is nothing of itself, but only an
abuse or travestie of good, so the evil age
exists not of itself, it is but the wrong side of
the good age. It is an abuse, a perversion, a
parody which degrades the idea of the Providence of God and His inspiration into the
utopias of the obstinate portion of the human
race.

Thus, when in the first ages of the Church,
the Christian doctrine shone forth like the sun,
and darted its light into all hearts, there
arose in the old world an antagonistic philosophy, which mimicked the Christian doctrine
for the purpose of opposing it. This philosophy derived its existence and strength wholly
from Christianity, which it perverted and
parodied. This was the evil age in opposition
to the good age.

So also, when God made known to His
Church that the moment was come for a mortal and decisive combat between truth and
error, the whole world heard His voice. The
old world, as well as the Church, saw that
blood must flow. Then the children of the

holy age shed their blood, and those of the evil age shed the blood of others. The evil age always works in contradiction to the idea with which God inspires the holy age: it reverses the idea of God. It slays, while the people of God are slain for the truth.

And in more modern days, after God had given to the world two such bright examples as St. Vincent of Paul, and Fenélon, the idea of God was so clearly put forth, that none could help understanding it. Love and charity: love for all mankind was then the inspiration of Providence. But the Church, or the holy age, saw the source of this love in the divine Heart of Jesus; and the perverse age, the evil and separated portion, found the source of this love in the affections of the carnal heart, boiling over with its own vicious passions. And whilst the Church adored the Sacred Heart of Jesus Christ, and looked upon it as her source of life, her model and centre, the perverse age came to adore two hearts which it is difficult to speak about.

Behold, on the altar of God, the nameless profanation of a woman's heart, gorged with dishonour! Behold another heart, the heart of a hangman gorged with blood, carried through the streets in a vessel of gold, with songs of triumph, as the Christian age carries in procession the Body and Blood of Jesus!

They rejected the worship of the Heart of Jesus and of the heart of Mary as superstitious, and they bow down before the heart of a harlot, and the heart of the greatest and most notorious of assassins! Behold the contrast

4

between the love of the wicked age, and the
love of the holy age !

But to come to the age in which we live.
What is the present inspiration of God ? What
is the divine idea which gives force and movement to the times in which we live ?   It is
not difficult to see it ; every eye sees it.   The
mission of this age is this :—God would have
this age carry out the second part of the law
in a greater degree than was done formerly.
The first part consists in loving God above all
things.   The second consists in loving one's
neighbour as oneself ; and this second commandment, says the Scripture, is like to the
first ; it is the same under another aspect.
Well, it is this aspect of the eternal law,
which God seems to wish especially to bring
before us.   He shows us the fields whitening
with their human harvest already ripe, and
He would make us see more and more clearly
what is the human harvest that we have to
gather in.   •

Let us consider and meditate, first of all
from another point of view, on this wonderful
truth.   I see that the idea which the age
ought to have and has, is the idea of the
grandeur and dignity of man ; and its inspiration is the love of mankind.   This is the idea
of the evil age, as well as of the good age.   Only
the holy age understands these things according to God and His Gospel, whilst the evil
age, as it always does, reverses the idea, and
destroys it by reversing it, and denies it while
asserting it.

What is the idea which this perverse age has

of the dignity of man ?   It thinks and declares
that human nature is pure, spotless, free from
original sin, without lawless desires, and impeccable, that its passions are perfections, its
deformities beauties, and that the works of
the flesh are holy.   Human nature, they say,
is divine, it is God !   Emancipate, then, this
enslaved God; let us emancipate ourselves from
faith, from law, and from conscience.   We
will no longer obey, but rule, we will reign by
the free and full development of our whole
nature, and of every one of its powers; and
this shall be the reign of God on earth.   This is a
true picture of the doctrine of these evil times;
and I now perceive that it is but a perversion
of God's revelation ill understood.

God wishes to raise us with a mighty hand;
He wishes to inspire us with courage, and
rescue us from the frightful debasement into
which the Christian soul has been cast by the
melancholy theology of the Protestants and
Jansenists. God wishes us to appreciate the
dignity and grandeur of human nature, notwithstanding its visible weaknesses and its
present misery.   For this purpose, He shows
us, by secret inspirations, and still more clearly
by the voice of the Church, through the
mouth of His vicegerent on earth, first of all,
that human nature is so noble, and so completely the image of God, that it is free—that
man is free to make and to choose his eternal destiny; that being evidently in a fallen
state—as we see—and having fallen by an act of
free-will, nevertheless the fall is not absolute,
but reparable; that in each soul, the fall is not

so entire, but that many noble powers still remain within it; that reason and liberty still dwell there, though in a feeble state; that the grace of God is ever pursuing each soul, and that the soul may correspond to it. But this is not all. The great truth which God proposes to our faith is that all mankind forms one whole, a single body, of which, as St. Paul says, we are all members. Leap for joy, then, ye men of every age; however humble they may be, let all members of this great body leap for joy. For its heart in some real sense is their own heart, and it has never been tainted with evil. The first heart of mankind, from which we all came, our first father and mother, were created immaculate. This first heart, or first couple, abused its freedom and sinned; and was replaced, or rather had been from all eternity in the foreknowledge of God, replaced by a heart still more free, but altogether sinless; it had been replaced by an atoning couple, which was to be, and which is the origin and the centre of our renewed nature, the life-giving spring of regenerated mankind. Leap for joy again, for this is not all; this second heart of the world, this second pair is not merely man filled with God's grace; in this second heart, the principal part is God Himself, God made man, and the secondary and inferior element of our universal heart is that sacred Vessel in which God was borne. In the mysteries of this great heart of the world, and which is thy heart too, O man, mankind, by one of its daughters, is Mother of God. Nay, more, human nature is united with God in the Incarnate-Son. Your Father, your own Father, the second Adam, is God Himself become man to be one of you, as Adam was one of you; and your own Mother, the second Eve, is Mother of God. Glorious in truth is the dignity of mankind, for its heart is God made man; and a woman made Mother of God. It is true, then, as this evil age asserts without understanding it, that human nature is altogether pure, spotless, without original sin, without concupiscence, sinless, and impeccable, that its divine emotions, love and pity, are perfections, that it has no deformity, that it is all fair, that its flesh is sanctified, sacred, and life-giving. Human nature is heavenly, for it is the Mother of God; human nature is divine, for it is the Man-God. Emancipate, then, this captive God; let us, with His aid, free ourselves from the yoke of our senses, from the bonds of the wicked world, from sin and from satan. Let us rebel against this external yoke, and obey nothing but our heart, our divine heart, that we may reign with Him. Let us reign by the free and full expansion of the whole life which He sends us, and of all its movements; and this will be the kingdom of God upon earth.

This is the inspiration of God, and the teaching of the generation of saints. This is what the generation of the wicked has been forced to teach after its own manner, repeating it almost word for word, but reversing its meaning. It calls our fall a triumph; our fall which every age can see, since evil and death are ours. It calls our deformities beauty, deformities so frightful, that without the supernatural aid of God, we cannot love one another. It sees vice, deformity, passion, corruption, concupiscence and pride, and calls them immaculate purity; this is what it calls God; but as for the true God-Man, it knows Him not; and as for the true Immaculate, the Mother of God, it will not hear of her. Thus does the generation of sinners imitate the generation of saints; it uses nearly the same words, it proclaims nearly the same hopes, but reverses everything. And yet under this perversion, we still recognize the idea which God gave us, the idea of the great dignity of mankind, and of the true worship of human nature. God indeed would inspire this age, with a greater love of mankind; He would inspire it, first, with a growing worship of adoration and love for the human nature of the God-Man; and then with a worship of veneration, of imitation, and of love for the pure human nature of the Immaculate Queen of the world, and Mother of God; and lastly, with a worship of compassion, love, and self-sacrifice for that poor sick and miserable human nature, which the Man-God has deigned to call His own body and His own suffering members.

Yes, I feel, and I see, that this is what God Himself at this time is teaching every watchful mind, every heart that is not frozen. So that even they who will not hear the Church, who do not believe the Gospel, who know nothing about the Mother of God, or the God-Man, even they may hear God whis-

pering to them, and importuning them within.
He speaks to their reason and their heart, and
says to them: Son of man, look on the earth,
and behold the sufferings of men, as they lie
in darkness and in death; is this thy whole
destiny, the destiny of mankind? dost thou
not wish something better? dost thou not see
how men sink down in endless degradation,
from want of loving Me and each other? but
thinkest thou that I love them not? thinkest
thou that human nature, with all its misery,
has no beauty? Beauty of souls! So great
is it, that one can and ought to love them
even unto death, as I do! Thy blood, O son
of man, thy heart, thy life, thy toil,—wilt
thou lend them to me for the service of mankind? dost thou understand me? human
nature can be raised up; am not I within it?
I am nearer to man than thou thinkest, for I
am one with him.

Thus it is that God seeks to inspire man
with faith in the Man-God, and in His Redemption; but the soul which is out of the
Church, not knowing how to interpret the
secret inspiration of God by the light of revealed doctrine, is startled and dazzled by the
closeness of God to man, and by the vivifying
force which He breathes into him. And if thou,
O Queen of ages, dost not come to her aid,
she will be led astray, she will confound God
with man, and will fall in with the evil age
instead of taking her side with Thy holy age.

But the inspiration goes further, and says:
No, all is not lost, O son of man! Raise thy
head, take courage. If mankind obeys Me, it

can do all. It can raise itself, by means of
My strength. It can do this, for it is free;
it can hear Me, conceive Me, bring me down
upon the earth: and this it has done. When
it is humble, pure, and obedient, it is My
Mother. "For whosoever shall do the will
of my Father, that is in heaven, he is my
brother, and sister, and *mother*." (Matt. xii. 50.)
And my mother is the most perfect of all
things that man can conceive, after Me. She
is absolutely without stain. Be bold, then, O
son of this Mother! Strive to be born in her
bosom, for this birth is left to thy choice, and
thou shalt become a brother of God, a son of
God.

Thus does God seek to inspire men with
faith in the supernatural new-birth, and in the
immaculate Mother of souls, who is the Mother
of supernatural life, the sole channel of the
new life, the life of God incarnate in our flesh.
But man, out of the Church, not being able to
elucidate the hidden inspiration by the light
of revealed doctrine, is dazzled by this divine
fellowship, by this wonderful beauty of humanity, which revelation makes known: and if
thou, O Queen of ages, dost not guide him, he
will go astray, he will pervert the meaning of
the divine inspiration, and will fall a victim to
the evil age.

But the revelation continues: Truly, O son
of man, thou must be born again, for thou
art full of misery, full of darkness, full of sin,
subject to evil and to death. Thou must be
changed; thou must know thine own blindness and misery; thou must be born again,

and become humble, pure, and chaste, and
during thy whole life thou wilt have to go on
fighting against those proud and sensual incli-
nations which keep thee at a distance from
Me.

This, then, is the crisis of the soul with
regard to the interior inspiration of God.
Here the soul must judge for herself, choose
her path, and take her place either in the
good or in the evil age. This is the moment
for thee to come to her aid, O Queen of ages.

If thou dost not come to her assistance, if
by reason of her natural habits and tendencies,
her instincts or her will, she chooses not to copy
thy virtues; if thy humility inspires her with
contempt; if thy purity frightens her and
makes her despair; if she will keep her pride,
and attach herself to her pleasures, she is lost,
and all the more certainly as she is the more
ready to obey the inspiration of the world.

Thus she upsets the twofold condition of
humility and purity, which God sets up; she
knows not, O Queen of ages, that immaculate
virginity alone is the Mother of God, and that
no one can receive and know God and the
God-Man but by thee, and she says: It is He
who speaks to me, I know it; He tells me
that He is near me, and in me, that human
nature is beautiful, and that it can do all
through Him. Therefore I am beautiful, I
bear God within me, and I can do all things.
And before long, intoxicated by this frightful
dram, compounded of God's inspiration, and
of its perversion by sin—sin, which the soul
has resolved to maintain to the last—stupified.

by this horrible mixture, man says: I am God;
we are gods. There is no such thing as evil.
We are immaculate. Human nature is God;
and that alone is to be adored.

This is the spirit of those prophets of the
evil age, who are now speaking to us;—a divine
inspiration in the midst of continued and reso-
lute sin. All is lost, the life of grace wasted,
the vessel broken, because the man has refused
to let himself be led to God by thee, O immaculate Queen of ages, who alone approachest God
by thine absolute purity.

But, when thou assistest this soul, O Queen
of ages, then if she does not spurn thy humility; if humility, purity, and chastity, have no
terrors for her; if from that time thou canst
hold her by the hand, and teach her to listen
and to obey like thee while God speaks, God
becomes immediately her Lord; He works in
her, He directs her; the soul no longer hesi-
tates between darkness and light.

The man sees what is darkness, and he sees
what is light. He sees his own misery, his
sin, and is seized with a holy hatred of it: he
sees the splendour of the light which is offered
to him, and is filled with a divine love for it.
He ceases at once to call darkness light, according to the word of Isaias. He no longer
says: "There is no evil, no sin," or "Evil is
only a smaller good." He no longer stifles
his heart and his conscience that he may deny
the existence of evil, nor does he lay aside his
reason to be able to deny that there is such a
thing as error. He no longer perverts the
divine inspiration which teaches him that the

Mother of life, the Mother of God and of souls, is altogether immaculate. He no longer concludes from this, in defiance of sense and reason, that mankind as a whole, such as it now is, is altogether immaculate. He sees evil within himself and outside of himself—the first condition for seeing the true good. And then notwithstanding the terrible aspect of present evil and of earthly sufferings, he will be able to raise his mind by faith, by love, and by hope to know or to believe what God inspires within and what the Church of God proclaims without; that there is a new world, that there is a new human nature, that the heart of this new nature is divine and immaculate, and that all souls by their free-will, under the bright and loving influence of this life-giving heart, may overcome evil and tend to its spotless purity, nay, even to its divinity.

Then does man understand the meaning of the words, "Regeneration of the world, deliverance of the nations, progress of the people, increase of light, liberty, love, life, and peace among men?" The soul no longer deceives herself, she understands her holy inspirations as God gives them, and not as the spirit of evil perverts them, to the confusion and destruction of everything.

Thou, then, O Mother of our souls, art truly the Queen of the age, for the idea of thee is its pole-star. Thy star has taught the age to glorify human nature and prove it immaculate; the eye sees this blessed star rise on the horizon but knows it not, though the Catholic Church cries aloud, Yes, the soft and brilliant

light of this blessed star is truly the light of
human nature, pure, virginal, and spotless,
Mother of God, Queen of ages, and of this
age.   But because you see this light, deny not
that darkness exists among men, but rather
fathom the depth of the darkness, and labour
to dissipate it by the light.

Thou, then, O holy Mother of God ! art
Queen of the present age, for thou art the star
which guides it.   Thou art the star which it
needs to guide it to God, to comprehend Him,
and to find Him in the thoughts which He
inspires.

O Queen of ages ! pray fervently for this
age ; suffer it not to deceive itself; put forth
thy whole strength, the whole might of thy
prayer.   O Queen—may I disclose thy mystery?   Thou prayest a double prayer ; thou
art the ladder of Jacob, by which angels ascend
and descend from earth to heaven, and from
heaven to earth.   This is the image of thy
prayer.   Thou prayest God to come down
from heaven, thou beseechest men to rise.
Thou prayest thy Son to knock at the door of
our hearts, and thou prayest our hearts to open
to Him ; O wonderful prayer of this tender,
this spotless Mother !   O my son, she says,
obey thy God, O my son, refuse not thy God.
Give our souls no rest, most holy Mother, thy
prayer is all-powerful with God, it is only too
often powerless with us.   But God gives thee
at this season a more piercing and a louder
voice ; cease not then, draw this whole age to
God ; persuade it to give itself up to God.

God would make mankind purer, freer, fairer, more lovely and more loving, let not this inspiration split the one age into two, into two jarring and contradictory ages, one destroying what the other would build,—let there be no evil age, let there only remain a holy age, or at least let the wicked age be weakened; let all upright hearts forsake it, let no power be given to it to seduce so many souls created for the light; let the wicked be its only followers, let numbers, courage, and enthusiasm, be found in the holy age, and let there be nothing to stifle the thoughts which God inspires for the progress of His kingdom upon earth.

MEDITATION XIII.

Queen of the age, pray for us!

Queen of the age, help us to go deeper into this fundamental idea!

Queen of the age, pray for the progress of God's kingdom upon earth!

"Our earth hath yielded its fruit," and its fruit, as the Church tells us, is the Incarnate Word. This earth, which brought forth thorns and thistles, has brought forth the most divine fruit which God could possibly create, the mature, the all-perfect, the heavenly and eternal fruit of infinite worth—the God-man. Pray, then, O holy Mother of God, for this earth which has yielded its fruit.

Pray that God's kingdom may come, and His will be done on earth as it is in heaven.

Is not this the special inspiration of God to the present age?

The evil age itself, O Queen of the holy age! is forced to recognize in its own fashion God's inspiration, and cries out more loudly than we, " Yes, let good reign on earth, let the earth become heaven:" but it adds, " Let there be no other heaven than this earth." Thus instead of raising earth towards heaven, it blots heaven out, and leaves earth hopeless to its darkness and its curse, and to the power of death and sin. But the Church of God, regenerated man, the holy age, of which thou art Queen, O Mother of God,—the Church which receives without mutilation the inspiration of God, points first to heaven, the world to come, the only world where there shall be no evil nor death, and where life, light, and love shall be changeless for eternity. And next, she tells men that if they will be humble and pure, if they will love God and one another, if they will unite their heart, their mind, and their life to the God-Man, by their conformity to the holy Mother of God, through whom God is born in the soul, they shall enter this eternal world ; and, moreover, shall draw down a blessing on the present world, and shall flood it with light and with grace, that shall make salvation easier for future ages.

But, further, does not the Catholic Church seem to have some great and special hope for the present time? does it not expect soon to see some striking progress of God's kingdom

on earth? Not that our great and patient
Church is one to share the blind hurry and
childish hope of those proud and sickly minds
that think they can reform the world the moment it will listen to them. She is not one to
accept as a prophecy the words of the holy
man who said that, "When the mystery of
the Immaculate Conception is defined by the
Church as a doctrine of faith, when the light
of this capital truth bursts forth in its magnificence, then shall the repose and peace of the
world be assured. But till that time we must
pray and suffer, and consent to see the world
remain in its present confusion." The Church,
though it honours this great man, does not
propose his words or his hope either to our
faith or to our pious belief.

But, on the other hand, are we forbidden to
believe that the world will some day be delivered from its present confusion? that man
will order the earth in justice and equity? that
he will rule it in peace? that the progress of
Christian wisdom will bring to pass this other
progress in the world? and that the progress
of wisdom will consist in a deeper humility
and a greater purity of soul; that is, in a
larger capacity for receiving God, and for wel-
coming His birth in our minds and in our
hearts? In other words, this progress would
consist in a more enlightened, more loving,
more true worship of imitation and of veneration for the holy Mother of God. And why
should not this progress of Christian wisdom
be helped on, when men come to understand it,
by the great act of the Church defining as a

dogma of faith the incomparable grandeur, and
the absolute purity of the holy Mother of God,
the Mother of regenerated mankind? That
the knowledge of the Mother of God should
have become clearer, that the worship now
paid her should be more profound in spirit and
truth, must surely be a sign of the present will
of God. Do we not see that God wishes at
this very time to draw us again more closely
to His divine Mother, that He may more
freely communicate Himself to men by means
of her, who everywhere and for ever gives Him
to the world?

Yes, the Catholic Church, represented by
its visible head, around whom all the suc-
cessors of the apostles congregate as one man,
the Church at the present moment seems full
of this hope. And who would dare to reproach
her for this, O my God? O if there was more
love for the visible representative of our Lord
Jesus Christ, if there was a firmer belief in the
Gospel, and in those words of our Master, "Thou
art Peter, and upon this rock I will build my
Church.....and I will give to thee the keys of
the kingdom of heaven;" if men were animated
and enlightened by these sentiments, would
they not look with greater respect towards this
man whom Jesus Christ has placed in the
centre of the world, in the centre of regenerated
mankind? Would they fail to meditate on
the measures he takes, on the words which
he addresses to the Church, as her teacher and
her head? Would they not discover therein
the present will of God, and the meaning of
the movements which He is impressing upon

the world? The Gospel says well that Caiphas prophesied because he was the high-priest. How should it not be so with him who is the high-priest of the new covenant, and who worships the divine King whom Caiphas crucified?

Thus we see the Vicar of Jesus Christ with his eyes fixed upon the whole Catholic world, (universum Catholicum contemplantes orbem,) like our Saviour in the Gospel, when "He saw men distressed and lying like sheep that have no shepherd." Thus we see him, like his Master whom he represents, uttering the profound grief which overwhelms him at the sight of the sufferings of the world, of the wars, of the civil discords, of the pests of the earth and of the air, which destroy men and overthrow cities. At this sight he raises his eyes to heaven, prays, and commands all men to pray and to supplicate without ceasing, (orare et obsecrare non desistinus,) and to ask God to put an end to all the wars in the whole world, to appease all divisions between the chiefs of the nations, to give peace, repose, and concord to Christian people, and to deliver them from all the ills which oppress them, and to bestow true prosperity upon them. These words are taken from the œcumenical letter which the visible representative of our Lord addresses to the world to exhort souls to a change of life, to penance, to pardon, and to good works, and to call upon man "to rejoice in hope."

Soon after the Sovereign Pontiff had pronounced these words, the consecration of the new basilica of St. Paul gave him occasion to repeat and exemplify them. He said: "That which we desire above all things in this solemnity, venerable brethren and dear children, is that all of you, with ourselves, in this most critical period for the Church and for Christian people, should not cease to implore with firm confidence the assistance of the great Apostle, that his prayers may obtain from God peace and repose both for the Church and for civil society; that evil may be vanquished, that all people may live in friendship in the unity of one faith; that all men may know our Lord Jesus Christ; that all may be penetrated with the same love; that all may ever work and meditate on all truth, all justice, all sanctity; that they may walk before God, always worthy of His sight, always filled with the fruit of good works, and that they may become heirs of eternal life."

When it pleased the Saviour to choose in these critical times, for His visible representative, this man of love, whose love is so little understood, all people blessed the first movements of his generous heart, which was inspired with the Spirit of his Master. From the first moment of his providential mission, he wished for a progress of God's kingdom upon earth; he sought to work out, in the humble patrimony which he had to govern, the experiment or rather the example of what he wished to give to the world: order, peace, and union in justice and truth. But his own understood him not. They first of all rent his garment, some trying to push him backwards, and others to cast him headlong over the precipice. Then they would have stoned him.

But, like the Saviour, he passed through the midst of them ; for his hour was not yet come. Seeing then, that he could not accomplish for one city (Urbi) the trial of his healing mission, he raised his eyes to heaven, and fixing them on the star of the ages and of saints, besought God to act for Himself, and to accomplish for the whole world (Orbi) the great blessing which He had for the moment refused to grant to the infatuated city. Then, still persevering in his prayer, and knowing well that God is always dispensing His gifts and bestowing His blessings, he turned to the Mother of mankind, and conjured her to teach the world how to listen, to accept and to obey. Then assuredly did God reply to His vicegerent on earth. The world must be ever more and more closely attached to the Mother of the God-Man, and thus shall His kingdom advance on the earth. And this is what has just been accomplished.

And with what prayers and hopes does the holy Pontiff conclude the apostolic letter in which he defines and proclaims the dogma of the Immaculate Conception ! These are the remarkable words in which our common Father solemnly declares the constant hope of his heart. " Yes, we have the sure hope, the full confidence that the ever blessed Virgin will obtain for us, by her powerful intercession, that the holy Church, our Mother, may triumph over all obstacles, and vanquish all error, and may be increased and developed in all places, and all nations ; that she may reign from one ocean to the other, and to the

very extremities of the world; that she may
reign in peace, calmness, and liberty; that
she may reign for the pardon of the guilty and
the healing of the sick; that every weary
heart may find strength, every afflicted heart
consolation, and every laden heart its defence,
and that all men may come forth from the
darkness in which they had lost themselves,
and may return to the way of justice and
truth, so that there should be but one flock
and one shepherd."

These are the hopes of the Catholic Church,
and of her visible head, the Vicar of Christ,
with regard to the present age.

Animated by the same hopes, and following
in the track of the Vicar of Christ, the present
Archbishop of Paris, in his Lenten Pastoral for
1859, says: " Lift up your eyes! Consider
the harvest of souls.......See what glorious
and holy undertakings are possible in these
days, not only immediately around us, but far
off, throughout the vast extent of the world
which seems to have entered on a decisive
crisis, either for its rise or fall. Nations are
brought together; the East and the West are
united. God seems to be raising the veil of
the future and showing us great things in store
for mankind!......Let us join unanimously in
the work of God, for the salvation of souls,
and by this union of hearts and minds, wonderful changes will soon take place in the
world!......Then the Church will cease to
moan, will open her heart to the liveliest
hopes, and witness a wonderful advance in
the propagation of the gospel and in the hap-

piness of mankind.   Then many mountains
of difficulties will be made smooth, many
chasms will be filled up, and men of expectation and desire will have a glimpse of the
realization of the kingdom of God upon the
earth."

Thanks be to God, that such are the hopes
of our pastors in the present day !

And why not hope ?   Why always refuse
to believe in great things, and in great novelties ?   O God, let not the world fall back into
the state of those souls who have given up the
idea of progress, and who say : I remain where
I am.   If nothing is more abominable to Thee
in one single soul, wilt Thou endure it in the
mass of mankind ?   No, Lord.   Thou hast
commanded us to repeat continually : "Thy
kingdom come, Thy will be done on earth, as
it is in heaven."   Give us the undying hope
and the undying will to fulfil, under Thine
inspiration and Thy guidance, the promises of
this holy prayer.   Grant that when we are
more united to this heavenly heart of human
nature, to this source of life, by which Thou
didst enter into the world to give life to the
world, we may then make use of Thy strength,
Thy inspirations, and Thy gifts to do also the
things that Thou hast done, O Lord, and
greater things still, according to Thy promise.

And does it not really seem, Lord, that
Thou speakest in a voice both clear and strong
to this age, and dost Thou not say to it, as
formerly to Thine apostles : "Behold, I say
to you, lift up your eyes, and see the countries,
for they are white already to harvest ?"   O

Jesus, is not this one of those manifestly divine words, which every mind and every heart is forced to hear in these days? Does not this wonderful word form part of the providential inspiration which is given now to the world, and perverted by the evil age, whilst. the good age meditates upon it and developes the divine seed which it contains?

"Others have laboured," again says the Saviour, "and ye have entered into their labours." The apostles gathered what the prophets had sown; but the apostles also sowed, and the Church has already gathered many times rich harvests of saints. And how is it we cannot see that we are on the eve of a harvest which will perhaps be the fairest of all?

For eighteen hundred years the earth has been sown with the divine seed; a seed which is never exhausted, but constantly puts forth fresh roots, and whose vigour is renewed by each recurring harvest. Now, more than ever, is the divine seed sown throughout the whole world. In the central portion of the globe, among Christian nations, it has already worked a great wonder. It nourishes and strengthens men with a divine food, and makes them rulers of the world. The ancient royal race of the earth was destroyed by barbarians, who were stronger than they. The new royal race has no barbarians to fear; all that does not belong to this race is hopelessly disabled. Christian nations united together, can dispose of the whole world as they please. For governing and regenerating the world, they have sciences, arts, discoveries, and all sorts of instruments which were unknown to former ages. These are the fruits of that strength of mind and will which the divine food imparts to them. The harvest then is manifestly ripe, and it is also a great harvest, for the whole world is the field which has to be reaped in these our times.

Lord Jesus! what is it, then, that is wanting for the beginning of such a splendid harvest? It is union. And Thou, O Lord, didst pray for union! "That they may be one, as we are one!" It was Thy last prayer; and in these days Thou art manifesting Thy desire to fulfil it. Thou art bringing us nearer to the heart of souls, to the heart of human nature, that heart which is made up of two hearts, as the human heart also ought to be: the heart which is the God-Man, and the Mother of the God-Man. Thou wouldst have us all united in this centre, around the visible Head of Thy Church.

Ah! if we would agree to a little more humility, a little more purity, our union would soon be blessed and confirmed. No doubt there will always be wicked and worthless hearts, incapable of loving; there will always be perverted minds that are enemies to the truth. But, under the all-powerful inspiration of God, the time may come for all active, influential souls, for those souls that think, that speak, and direct, to find themselves in an overwhelming majority for Christian objects. Is it not evident that at such a time the thought of Christian unity, fortified by the wonderful appliances which add a hundredfold to its strength, and which transport men with the quickness of light, will encircle the whole world as with a net? Then shall the sheaves be brought to thy feet, O Queen of the age, Mother of regenerated mankind.

O my Queen, pray God to give me the grace to become one of thy reapers. The harvest is great, and the labourers few. But how can men, with their eyes open, stand idle? For my part, O Mother of the age, I offer thee all my strength and the labour of my whole life. Long enough have I wasted my days, in barren toils which will not save one soul, which will not dry up one tear, and will not secure for miserable men one single ear of the harvest. Now, I know the object and the end of the work. My heart shall find its joy in this labour; happy shall I be if with Jesus I can say when called to the tribunal of God: "Lord, I have finished the work which Thou hast given me to do."

MEDITATION XIV.

Queen of doctors, pray for us!

Queen of doctors, pray for us, and as we desire to serve God in spirit and in truth, and also to honour thee in our minds and in our hearts, obtain for those amongst us whose understanding is open to the light, the happiness of sharing some of those sublime ideas which led Thy holy doctors in all ages to maintain with zeal the dogma of Thine Immaculate Conception.

If we ask what God is, these doctors tell us, He is that being than whom nothing greater can be conceived. So that, to form some idea of God, there is a way as simple as it is sure—to heap together in our thought the idea of every possible perfection, raised to the highest conceivable degree. We may give the reins to our heart, our reason, and our fancy, but we shall never rise high enough, and when we have thought of the most perfect, the most wonderful, the most lovely, the most adorable being that we can conceive, let us still say, this is nothing, God is infinitely more perfect than anything we can conceive. This is the teaching of all Christian doctors, and all philosophers, and their arguments on this head are as certain and as solid as the infallible proofs of geometry.

In the same way the doctors tell us there is a created being, the image of God, whose perfection may in some sense be always growing till it is bounded by nothing short of infinity; and this creature, the pure image of God, possesses a purity than which no greater can be conceived except God's.

This is St. Anselm's idea,—he it was who said, God is the being than whom nothing more perfect can be conceived. He it is who says of the holy Mother of God; She is the

5

creature than whom nothing more pure can
be conceived except God.*

And St. Thomas, the greatest of philosophers and of theologians, thus unfolds St.
Anselm's idea.   Purity, he says, is the absence of all spot; hence it is possible that a
creature may exist, than whom it is impossible to conceive anything purer amongst creatures ; it is enough that this being should not
have a single spot, and that no sin should
ever have stained her.   Such is the purity of
the Blessed Virgin, who was free from all sin,
actual or original.   Only her purity is not
equal to God's, because she had the power of
sinning, which God could never have.   But if
we speak of the goodness of a creature, adds
St. Thomas, since goodness is measured by its
approximation to the sovereign Good, which
is infinite, it follows that a goodness greater
than any created goodness, is always possible.

St. Thomas, we see, here teaches the whole
truth, and resolves the whole doubt.   Only in
his answer he says something which, ill-
understood, may shock the ears of Christians.
He seems to say that the Virgin has all conceivable purity, but not all possible goodness.
But he only means, that her perfection may
be ever growing without ever equalling God's,
and that her brightness is not that infinite
light, or infinite glory, which is God.   The
Queen of heaven, clothed with the sun, clothed
with Him who is the only well-spring of the

* Quâ major sub Deo nullatenus intelligitur.—*Bull of Pius
IX.*

brightness, the light and the love of saints, shines like the sun, as our Saviour said that the saints shall shine like the stars. But, does the sun itself fill infinite space with its light? Surely not. There was a time when its rays did not even reach the earth; they soon traversed millions and millions of times this distance; but still they have a limit. This limit may recede with the rapidity of lightning, or almost of thought, but a limit it will ever remain. The sphere of the sun's radiance is ever increasing with majestic strides, but it must ever have its measure and its bounds. So it is with the brightness of the saints and the glory, or as St. Thomas calls it, the goodness of the Blessed Virgin.

And besides, in another place, St. Thomas confesses that God could not have created anything more holy than the Blessed Virgin, and the humanity of Jesus Christ. "The humanity of Jesus Christ," says he, "as being one with God,—and the Virgin as being the Mother of God,—have a sort of infinite dignity imparted to them by the infinite Goodness, which is God; in this sense nothing better can be created, for there is nothing which is better than God." (1. q. xxvi. art 6. ad 4.) From this we may understand in what sense the doctors of the Church affirm that there is one creature in existence than whom nothing more perfect, nothing more pure can be conceived.

In this sense, then, according to them, there exists in the centre of creation the highest degree of beauty and perfection with which it

was possible for God to endow finite beings.
Let us not say that God might have created a
better world, but that He did not so will,
without at the same time laying down the
necessary restrictions of the angelic doctor.
Let us rather say that He might have created
one less beautiful, but that He did not so will.
He might first of all have left man to his own
nature, and not have raised him by grace to a
participation of the divine nature. He might
not have pre-ordained the birth of a daughter
of Adam, who, though of the human race,
should yet be without spot. It would have
been changing the plan of the universe, I
know, but this plan might have been changed;
in this case there would not have existed
any mere creature than whom it would be
impossible to conceive one more pure. But
this was not the will of God. He chose that
His work should have this seal of perfection,
that the human understanding and the human
heart should not seek in vain anywhere short
of God for the purest of all possible beauty.

This is why these doctors uphold with so
much zeal the opinion that there exists one
creature without spot, and that the Queen of
the universe, the Mother of God, who is necessarily, of all the works of God, the most perfect after the humanity of Jesus Christ, is also
the perfection of beauty without any spot or
fault. That she is pure and spotless in her
life, pure and spotless in her heart, wherein
concupiscence never dared to raise its head;
that she is pure and spotless in her birth and
in her conception. Without this doctrine, it

would seem that the last link of the golden chain which is to reunite all creation to the throne of God and to the incarnate Word would be wanting.

It is good for me, O my God, that my soul should dwell on these ideas of perfection, that it should believe firmly and constantly that all excellence and all beauty exist in Thee in an infinite degree, and further, that in Thy creation, and in this our human nature, there exists a higher degree of beauty and excellence than it is possible for us to conceive.* When we think of Thee we must add infinity to our conceptions. When we think of Thine immaculate image we must not add infinity to it, but we must enlarge our ideas to the utmost, and be convinced that it is far more beautiful than we can imagine. O my God, since the world is so beautiful I will be no longer sad. I will correct in myself this want of admiration, of veneration, and of enthusiasm, which is one of the greatest deformities of the carnal man. I will wean myself and others, as far as I can, from this fatal and detestable habit of the so-called prudent and experienced, which consists in stifling all lofty aspirations, and trusting only to grovelling thoughts. Low thoughts, I know, correspond for our short day with the contemptible realities which surround us, but high thoughts correspond to the holy realities

---

* ...."Tota pulchra et perfecta eam innocentiæ et sanctitatis plenitudinem præ se ferret, qua major sub Deo nullatenus intelligitur, et quam præter Deum nemo assequi cogitando potest."— Apostolical Letters of Pius IX.

of heaven and of God, and of His immaculate
and well-beloved creature, our Mother and our
Hope, the heavenly centre which attracts all
the warmth, all the force, and all the glory of
the soul to restore them to God from whom
they come.

MEDITATION XV.

Mother, most admirable, pray for us!

Mother most admirable, whose beauty we
have come to understand by meditating on the
Holy Scriptures and the writings of the
Fathers and Doctors of the Church; Virgin,
whom we have found inferior to none but God,
pray for us; pray for the whole Church, that
in these times, and that soon, thy power may
shine forth in some brilliant manifestation!

And in what does the power of thy surpas-
sing beauty principally consist, if it is not in
destroying all heresies, that is, in conquering
that principle of apostasy and pride, which
divides men and retards the period of their
union amongst themselves and with God by
means of light and love?

And what ray of light and love can dry up
the intellectual source of heresy, if not the
clear exposition of the mystery of the Immaculate Mother of God?

The mystery of the Mother of God carrying
her Son, either in her bosom or in her arms,

is manifestly the focus of truth, the centre of all questions between God and man, and the point of contact between God and the world.

The mystery of the connection between God and the world, which is the perpetual meditation of every mind which rouses itself from the general slumber, has been at all times the spring of the most contradictory errors and heresies. Now the mystery of the Immaculate Mother of God, carrying her Son either in her womb or in her arms, contains the answer to them all.

Let us, therefore, meditate on what the Catholic Church, the depository of all truth, offers to our veneration and our contemplation. This is—the God-Man, the Son of God, conceived by the Holy Ghost; the God-Man as an infant, the God-Man borne in the arms of His ever-immaculate creature, notwithstanding the fall of the first man; the God-Man borne in the arms of His Mother, of a Mother who merited to be the Mother of God, of a Mother whose soul and body were worthy to bear God; the God-Man as a child, thus borne in the arms of His Mother, in the midst of a fallen world, to save it, and to uplift the creature to its eternal and unchangeable perfection.

Yes, all heresies are overcome by the light of this central dogma, by this fulness of truth, by this true Sun from whose rays no error can be hidden.

Jesus, God and man, send forth Thy light and dissipate the frightful darkness of those minds that have lost sight of God, that see nothing be-

yond man alone, and that say there is neither
soul nor God in the world.   Thou who art truly
God and truly man, God clothed with humanity, with a human soul and a human body,
enlighten these blind eyes that they may see
behind the forms of body the free and spiritual soul, and behind Thy clothing of body
and of soul afford them a glimpse of the infinite glory of Thy Godhead.

O Jesus, true God and true man, send
another ray and dissipate the frightful darkness of those minds that have lost sight of
God, that call this body and this human soul
which they see divine, that call everything
God.   Show them Thy humanity, which is
infinitely distinct from Thy divinity, and
subject to infirmity and to death ; show them
Thy growth, which is that of human nature,
and not of the eternal and immutable Divinity,
which cannot grow.   Show them, outside of
Thyself, the fallen world which has to be saved,
this limited, transitory, and imperfect world,
which has to be brought to perfection and to
eternal life.

O Jesus, true God and true man, who
unitest in Thy person two natures infinitely
distinct, send again a ray and dissipate the
frightful darkness of those minds which are
fully persuaded that the world is not God, and
that this world has been created by God, and
yet believe not in any further connexion of
God with the world, and which see this world
as it were separated by infinity and eternity
from the infinite God.   Show them, O Jesus,
the creature and the Creator united in the

unity of Thy divine Person; show them that
we not only breathe, live, and have our being
in God; that God not only upholds each
atom of creation by His Word and by
His power; that God not only sustains every
thing that has being, vivifies all that lives,
acts in each movement, works in each action, and governs by His Providence the
whole universe, nay, each atom of the universe
with the same care as the whole; but show
them also that this natural presence of God,
whereby He is present in all parts of His work
by His essence and His power, is nothing in
comparison to the supernatural union of God
with the soul by His divine grace, which itself is
but a small thing compared to the substantial,
absolute, hypostatic union between the divine
and human nature in the person of the Word.
Show them Thy love, O my God, Son of God
and Son of man, which surpasses, in the supernatural power of Thine embrace, all possible union between created béings, and that of
all the ties of blood; that of the husband and
wife, of the son and mother, that of souls
united in love, and that of the soul with its
own body. Show them, O God, whether it
be true that Thou art a God without love, a
God separated from the world. Show them
Thy divinity united to Thy humanity. Show
them,.O Word Incarnate, who wast borne by
Thy Immaculate creature, show them the
Mother who carries Thee, walking in this valley
of tears and holding God in her arms.

O Jesus, divine Infant, borne by Thy
Mother, send another ray and dissipate the sad

darkness in which those minds are buried who
are without hope! Look on the poor infidels!
Look on those Christians who are asleep!
Show them the Word Incarnate, as an Infant
in the arms of His Mother, and growing up
unto the perfect man. Show them that therein is found the whole meaning of the history
of mankind, and the whole meaning of the
history of each soul, the whole plan of God's
work, whether in the individual soul or in
all mankind. Banish the spirits of darkness,
and the dim fancies which make them see the
work of God as if it were stricken with barrenness and inaction, in misery and evil, and
which give them up in their despair to indolence, to the present enjoyment, and to the
deadly torpidity of the senses. Thy work is
holy, O my God ! This world even, our temporary abode, is holy, it is Thy footstool, for it
is the pedestal of the divine Mother who bears
Thee in her arms.

Remedy the utterly desperate case of those
of whom Isaias speaks, " who shall not have the
morning light, who shall pass through the
light without knowing it, who shall curse
their King and their God, and shall look up-
wards; and they shall look to the earth and
behold trouble and darkness, weakness and
distress;" remedy also the less desperate case
of those who do not pray that Thy will may
be done on earth as it is in heaven, who do not
seek it on earth, and still less expect it in
heaven; who know not that there is a divine
progress on the earth, a plan of salvation for
all people, a divine progress in the world and

in each soul, a growth of the Man-God, in the midst of His creation, till it shall grow up unto the perfect man.

Yes, O Infant Jesus, Thou God-Man, who didst increase in grace and in wisdom before God and before men, till Thou hadst grown up unto the perfect man, in this human nature which has been saved and exalted by Thee, give unto men the hope of seeing God born in them, growing in them, purifying them, glorifying them. Give them the hope of one day seeing the new heaven and the new earth in which justice shall dwell, and of which Thou wilt be the life, the light, and the happiness. Give them the hope of seeing the will of God accomplished on earth as it is in heaven, by Thy increase throughout the whole human race, before God and before men.

O Jesus, who art carried in the arms of Thine immaculate creature, send forth another ray to disperse the horrible darkness wherein those sombre seekers into the secrets of evil are plunged, and are still plunging, who contemplate the night, either because they love darkness and evil, or because they fear them and believe them to be greater than, or at least equal to, Thee. They think they see that good and evil share the world like night and day, they attribute to evil a majesty which it has not, and worship the principle of darkness as much as, or more than, the principle of light. Others, without believing that Thy enemy is stronger than Thou, think that all beings are bad from the roots, and that the principle of life is changed into the poison of hell. They think that God was conquered for a time by sin, that His whole work fell from His Hands, and that it is only by an immense effort that He has been able to collect together its fragments once more. There are, even among people calling themselves Christians, those who magnify the power of evil; attributing to it, in spite of the Church, a majesty which it has not, and who suppose that it entered into everything, even for an instant into the Mother of God, so that there remained not for mankind one spark, one germ of supernatural life. They think that evil has been permitted to destroy in the soul all trace of freedom and of reason; that our will is completely enslaved and can work nothing but evil, that our intelligence is completely enfeebled, and sees nothing but error, and that there remains nothing in the soul of the children of Adam which is not irrevocably cursed. These terrorists of religion attribute to God a fatal predestination, and an everlasting and arbitrary will to deceive and bring to perdition the multitude of souls. According to them man can neither see nor act, and this slave who can do nothing, this dupe who can see nothing, it is God's pleasure to lead to perdition, and to give up the poor victim of evil to the eternal torments for which he was created.

O Jesus! from Thy throne in the arms of Thine Immaculate Mother, show them how Thou hast from all eternity saved from evil this Mother of all men, this principle of regenerated mankind, how evil was never permitted to reach Thy heaven, the very crown and core of Thy creation. In this paradise of the new Adam, in this august and divine world of God, Thy will has always been done; and the two royal Souls, Thine own and that of Thy Mother, the souls of the bridegroom and the spouse, of whom all the elect were to be born, have ever had their foot on the head of the serpent. Thine Immaculate Mother, trampling evil under foot and bearing her Divine Son in her arms, has ever been the eternal idea and the fixed centre of Thy creation; Thou didst call the darkness "outer," and it has ever been external to Thy Mother.

Finally, O most holy Virgin! who bearest thy divine Son, send forth thy light to overcome those great heresies which still bear sway among so many nations, which protest even in these days against the Church and against thee. Enlighten, O Jesus! those who have no feeling of unity, who believe Thy Church to be divisible and capable of living, like the sections of a worm, after it is cut up. Enlighten those who know not tradition. Enlighten those who believe not in the continual presence of the Holy Spirit in the Church. Enlighten those who believe not in Thy reign on the earth, and who attribute Thy power to temporal sceptres; those who know not the excellence of virginity, and still less of humility, and who attribute to each member the continual inspiration of the Spirit, which is promised to the entire body; those who will have no other expiatory sufferings than those which Thou hast suffered, and who understand not with St. Paul that they

should themselves fill up those things that are
wanting of Thy sufferings; those who believe
not in the merit of man's labour, in the merits
of his free will, and of his works, and who
ignore all the human side of the redemption.
Let all such look on thee, O divine Mother,
thou who hast merited to be the Mother of
God, and by whom we have merited to receive
within us the source of life;* let them look on
the God-Man, who came into the world through
thee, by thy consent; let them contemplate
thee at the foot of the cross, uniting thyself to
the sacrifice, and offering up the Flesh of thy
flesh and the Blood of thy blood; may they
understand thy perfect and profound personal
sacrifice of a spotless virginity and boundless
humility, both necessary for the conception of
God; may they look upon thee, O Mother of
the whole Church, in whom all the living
members of the Church, have but one heart
and one soul—thy heart and soul, O Mother of
God, united to the heart and soul of Jesus;
may they look up to thee who alone didst
conceive by the Holy Ghost, to whom alone
His grace is given, and to those who are joined
to thee, as the grain of wheat to the ear; may
they look towards thee, O Queen of the world,
whose Son sustains the world on His sceptre,
which is the cross; and may they understand
that thou art also the Mother most admirable,
the focus of truth, and the necessary link of
unity.

Such, O Mary, is the greatness of thy

* Per quam meruimus Auctorem vitæ suscipere.

power. By thy immaculate purity, and by thy divine Son whom thou wast worthy to bear, thou dost alone exterminate all heresies throughout the world, from the great and primitive heresy against which thou didst defend the heart of human nature—the heart of God's work, to all those heresies which have sprung from it, and which labour to divide the Church. All heresy springs partly from pride of heart, partly from an insufficiency or exaggeration of thought. The mind exaggerates one side of the truth, and so destroys the other. Thou then, who art not only humility itself, but also through the divine Son in thine arms, the focus, the centre, the union of all truth, how shouldst thou not be the glorious destroyer of all heresies? Those who see nothing but God in the creature, and those who see no God therein; those who see no evil in it, and those who see nothing but evil, those who adore evil, and attribute it to God, those who deny it, and those who fear it more than they fear God; those who see nothing but man, and those who place the wicked in the kingdom of God; those who deliver to eternal flames nearly the whole of the human race; those who would have sin which is not personal expiated in eternal torments, and who are called in theology *tortores infantium;* those who deny the necessity of Christian warfare and sacrifice, and of the cross; those who see nothing higher than human nature, and those who think it essentially accursed, all these have only to look on thee, O Mother of God, and His immaculate master-piece, crushing the head of the serpent, and carrying in-thy arms the God-Man, the divine Infant, who holds in one hand the world surmounted by a cross. God, man, and the world and their relations; liberty, sin and its limits; the supernatural union of God and the world; the victory over evil, the conflict, the sacrifice, the labour, the cross, the salvation of the world, all this is seen in thy image, Mother most admirable, who bearest thy Son in thine arms, and in Him possessest the assemblage of all truths.

Let this be thy petition, O Mother most admirable, that Jesus may grow in thy arms, and that the ever increasing manifestation of thy mysteries may enkindle in an increasing number of hearts this spark of truth, this first glimpse of heaven, this star of which the apostle St. Peter says to the Christians: "Ye do well to attend to the prophetical word, until the day-star arise in your hearts." Then will be realised St. Paul's words, "Until we all meet in the unity of the faith, and of the knowledge of the Son of God, unto a perfect man, unto the measure of the age of the fulness of Christ: that henceforth we be no more children tossed to and fro, and carried about with every wind of doctrine by the wickedness of men."

Now I understand why Catholic piety every where multiplies pictures of the Immaculate Mother holding her divine Son in her arms: it is this image that brings before us all truth under its most pleasing aspect. May God be

praised that He designs to spread the truth by
this means! A little picture drawn by the
humblest artist, brings the whole Christian
creed before the weakest understanding. The
poorest woman, before her Madonna, sees how
much God loves us, and in what manner He
dwells among us. She sees God so closely
united to man, that He is Himself man. She
sees Him borne by His creature, fed by her in
His human nature. She understands the word
of St. Paul: "Glorify, and bear God in your
body." She understands that it is a creature
who is a virgin, without spot, immaculate,
who conceives God, bears Him and nourishes
Him. She · believes in uncreated perfection,
and in created perfection. By the contrast,
she knows her own sin and weeps for it, but at
the same time she sees Him who redeemed it
and blotted it out; hope springs up from her
sorrow; she believes in heaven, in the eternal
possession of God, in eternal life, the image of
which she has before her eyes. Yes, Lord, so
it has seemed good to Thee! Thou hast revealed these things to the lowly and the humble
of heart, while the learned are yet seeking
them. And now, Lord, I will ever love and
meditate upon this holy picture, I will dis-
tribute it and make it known. Inspire the
pencil or the chisel of some Christian artist, to
embody a type better than the best we have,
for all fall short of thy heavenly beauty. And
above all, bless my mind, and my imagination,
my mental mirror, that I may bear therein the
image of the immaculate Mother, and of her
divine Child, but an image more heavenly,

more lively, more gentle, and more compassionate, than any painter here below can represent it. Happy are those among Thy saints, O Jesus! who, while yet on earth, have seen more than the picture!

———

MEDITATION XVI.

Holy Virgin of virgins, pray for us!

Pray for us, Virgin of virgins, that some share in thy virginity may be given to us, that we may also be virgins, in thee, and with thee, and that thou mayst indeed be " the Virgin of virgins" for us.

The chaste soul, is a soul without any trace either of pride or of sensuality; it is a soul which neither exalts nor debases herself, but holds herself in her own place, in the centre in which God has created her, and in which He desires to sanctify her.

O Mary! thou alone art altogether a Virgin. Neither in thy person, nor in thy free will, in thy nature, in the invisible depths of the soul which God only can see, in thine immaculate body, nor in those deep abysses of the animal nature, in which the will has no part, of which the mind understands nought, hast thou ever had the least trace, the least beginnings of pride or of sensuality. Thou alone hast never exalted thyself, nor debased thyself; thou alone didst never wander from that position which the Eternal Will had assigned to us, and which is the centre from whence He gives life, light, heat, fruitfulness, and peace to His creature.

All other souls have lost their primordial virginity; all have either been lifted up or cast down; all have left their place, and the position which God assigned them; all have gone astray, have banished themselves, have been wanderers from the divine Centre and well-spring of life.

What do I say? Can a creature go astray from God? Is He not essentially present in every place, in every atom of matter, in every individual soul? "No," says St. Augustine, "we cannot be far from God in space, but only in will." "God," says St. Teresa, "like a fixed sun, is always in the very midst of the soul," but, adds this gifted woman, who perhaps of all the saints had the deepest knowledge of the soul, "if God is there, we are away; our heart is not there." The centre and well-spring of the life which we cut out for ourselves is not in union with the centre and well-spring of the life which God gives or would give us.

St. Teresa elsewhere says, "Our soul, whose greatness is incredible, may be likened to a castle surrounded with seven walls. In the midst of them all God sits waiting for us, while around the seventh wall, outside the castle, we, who never enter into ourselves, are marching like sentinels who never go inside the palace gates, and know only its ditches and its walls."

But how imperfect are these comparisons,

to show us the state of the fallen soul! The
soul, so much more beautiful, so much grander
than castle or palace could be !

Might we not rather compare the fallen soul
to a planet wandering far from its sun, and
receiving only its distant and diminished rays,
superficially and one-sidedly? A planet whose
light is never full, always needing increase,
but always decreasing the moment it reaches
its meridian ; a banished wanderer, always
changing from darkness to light, and from
light to darkness, from the fruitfulness of sum-
mer to the barrenness of winter, whose fruitful
zones are squeezed up between two icy poles,
and separated by torrid tropics; a ·planet
which, like ours, is always seeking in its perpetual revolutions the place of its eternal repose—is not this the best image of the soul?

Thus the abode of man would be the truest
symbol of the state of his soul.

But these comparisons fail the moment we
come to the supernatural regeneration of the
soul, that wonderful change, whose greatness
no man knoweth. To carry out the comparison, we ought to know what the world will
be like after it has been transfigured by fire,
and changed into the new heavens and the
new earth, where justice shall abide; or
else we ought to rise above our earth, and
ascend to the luminary of which it is said:
" God hath placed His tabernacle in the Sun."
And again: " The woman was clothed with
the Sun." There we have already found the
glorious image of Mary, the image of the
Virgin of virgins, who surrounds on all sides

the source of life, who receives the fulness of His gifts, and who, without change of season, or alternations of night and day, is clothed and glorified, enlightened and fertilized with a mighty aureole of light and fire. Souls in a state of grace, but not yet glorified, are in an intermediate condition; they are above the earth, which only receives its light from without with many a change, and they are far below that orb which bears in its bosom the source of light, and which imparts it to the planets. They will only become like it, when according to the divine promise, they shall shine like stars in the firmament.

What, then, is the condition of the soul in the state of grace, but still militant? This soul, if I may say so, is like a sun in the course of formation.

It has already become self-luminous, but its light is weak, because the imperfections of the soul extinguish nearly all its rays. It has the power of luminosity, but its light has as yet no brilliancy, no expansion, no strength.

And why? because it has not as yet thy maternal virginity, O Virgin of virgins.

The faith teaches us that the soul, though in a state of grace, nevertheless, throughout this life, ever bears within herself the source of concupiscence along with the source of life; she bears within her those darksome pits of the concupiscence of pride, and of the concupiscence of sensuality, whose effects and strength are constantly varying with each motion of free-will, and which are like the two arms of Satan, embracing the source of grace, like those two

frightful arms wherewith the Devil carried the
Lord to the top of the mountain to tempt
Him. The soul bears within herself this Sun
of justice, but with it also the roots of sin,
sources of darkness which will seek to extinguish the source of light. This soul, still so
far removed from thy virginity, O Virgin of
virgins, will perhaps give herself up to her
evil desires, and like the old people of God,
will despise, reject, and crucify Him who
comes to save her, to exalt her to heaven, to
fill her with radiance, and to make her like a
bright-shining star. But perhaps she will
unite herself to Him who is the source of light
and life, and borrow from Him such brilliancy
and such heat, that she will ascend to the
heavens and there shine like a star.

A star in the course of formation, is like a
soul in which darkness and light are waging
war with one another.

But how, O Mary, can this heavenly star
either develop itself to perfection, or fall for
ever out of heaven, and tumble like a dark
mass through space? In proportion as she
comes nearer, or goes farther from thee, O
Virgin of virgins, she either develops or falls
away—in proportion as she borrows from thee
the power of kindling and radiating light.
But the power of kindling and implanting
luminosity in the soul is virginity,—virginity,
either original or recovered.

O Mary, Virgin of virgins! look down on
thy children, the daughters of Jerusalem, the
souls in which the sin of Adam has destroyed
original virginity ; look on those whose own

personal and actual sin, superadded to original sin, has destroyed their personal virginity; but who, either by baptism or penance, have received again the source of light and grace, that is to say, God Himself. These souls must now be made like to Thee, in order to become living tabernacles of God. The Word is being born in them, and says to thee: "O Mother of God, dwell in those souls, and spread thy roots in the midst of them. Thou didst conceive Me, for thou alone wast worthy, thou alone didst merit it; thou hast nourished Me, fed Me at thy bosom, carried Me in thy arms, hast watched over Me till I enlightened the world, and overcame death. Now, O my only Mother, Mother of the elect, make Me grow also in these souls, do thou fashion Me, and bring Me to perfection in them."

But how can this be? I can well understand that God, who can do all things, who is everywhere, whose presence pervades everything, can come into any soul; but how can the Blessed Virgin come into my soul? How shall she dwell in me, and I in her? How shall she spread her roots in my soul, as Holy Scripture expresses it?

The way is this. God has said: "Woe to him that is alone!" and in another place: "Where there are two or three gathered together in my name, there am I in the midst of them;" and again: "They shall have but one heart and one soul." The will of God is, in one sense, that the whole multitude of souls should be but one. The work of God is neither a cloud of dust, nor a heap of sand. His new creation must be love and union itself. The union of each grape in the unity of the bunch, or of each grain of corn in the unity of the ear, is but a feeble expression of the union of souls in the heavenly city. What is this city, if thou art not it, O Virgin of virgins, with thy Son in thine arms? Who is this vine? Thou also, united to Him. Who is the sacred ear of corn, if not thou, of whom it is written : " Thy womb is like a heap of wheat?"

To thee, then, we must turn, O sacred tabernacle, wherein God abides ; we must be joined to thee, we must live in thee, O Mother of the Church of God. Like living grains of wheat, we must each be united to thee, who art the " heap." As each flower and each fruit is visibly attached to the stalk that bears it, and as this link is the canal by which the plant nourishes its fruit with its sap, so the soul, regenerated in God, must be joined to the Mother of grace, the heavenly Jerusalem, by a real and living link, by a channel of grace which issues from her bosom, and reaches even to the soul. This is the meaning of Scripture, when it says : " He that made me rested in my tabernacle, and said to me, Let thy dwelling be in my people, and take root in my elect." (Eccles. xxiv. 13.) By this sacred channel the blood of Christ comes to the soul, and gives increase to the Word, which it makes incarnate therein.

But, O Virgin of virgins! all has not yet been said. More than this is needed for a soul to become Mother of the Word, according to the text, " Whosoever doeth the will of my

Father, he is my brother, my sister my mother." It is not enough for the Holy Spirit to have drawn the fallen soul; it is not enough for Him to have begun dwelling in this soul, now re-united to the Church; it is not enough that He should infuse His unction into this soul through the centre of unity, through the heart of the Mother of the elect, and thus begin to form Jesus Christ in this soul; the soul must also allow the divine man to grow within her, and must not destroy by her crimes the divine fruit which the Spirit of God is forming in her.

Here it is that the strife of grace against sin, and of sin against grace, is chiefly manifested. Here the free soul may raise herself to heaven, by her labours and her merits, and by her attention to the light within her, or may fall headlong into the abyss if she quenches it by her sin. And all depends upon the progress which the soul can make in the attainment of spiritual virginity. Will she attain, O Virgin of virgins, to the state of unity with thee? Will she learn to imitate more and more perfectly thy heavenly state, to the utter extinction of the flames of concupiscence? Will she annihilate them by the might of the divine flame of love that dwells in her? or will she allow them ever in their sacrilegious banquets to glut themselves like devils even with the Spirit of God, and the Blood of Jesus Christ?

O Virgin of virgins! give thy mighty aid to the soul in conflict. Obtain for her that inextinguishable hatred which God in the

6

beginning placed between thee and the power
of the enemy; let the touch of thy hands and
of thy maternal heart give her purity that she
may rise, and humility that she may be recollected. Let her have but these two virtues,
and the love of God will immediately raise
her from the baseness of sensuality, and abase
the contemptible high-mindedness of pride.
These criminal flames which waste away the
soul, which divide our heart, and make our
heart double, and our life wrong either way,
whether in fancying ourselves raised to an
equality with the angels, or in descending to
the level of the brutes,—these two springs of
evil are dammed up by the power of love.
The soul regains her virginity in thee and by
thee, O Virgin of virgins! The light of truth
and holiness, the pure and sacred fire which is
rekindled in the centre of the soul, and is fed
by her powers in proportion as they abandon
the springs of pride and sensuality,—her light
and her fire then concentrate themselves in
her; the spark increases into a brighter and
stronger flame: the soul, released from those
darkening influences, generates ever-increasing
light and heat; the brightness of the eternal
light penetrates, traverses, and envelops her;
the star is formed in holiness, to become one
day in heaven a star in thy crown, O Virgin
of virgins!

Yes, my God, I have often felt in my soul,
and I may say even in my body, these two
forces of deadly energy, one of which degrades
me, while the other puffs me up; one famishes

nie and the other intoxicates me. O how often have I felt that immoral hunger of sensuality, which wastes away our life, and that drunken pride of the intellect, which makes our life vanish like smoke! What is it that wastes? it is the heart. Whenever a life consumes itself in the furnace of concupiscence, the heart is empty; its love, its heat, its energies, its courage and its hopes, all disappear; its fire, at once purifying, humble and mighty, because it is concentrated, is all extinguished, and nothing is left but dust and ashes. Is not this the meaning of the prophet, " Their heart is nought but ashes?" Yea, Lord, it seems that my soul has become like this, emptiness within, fever and flame without. It seems that my body and soul can only escape this state by death.

Was it not, O Lord, to transform our soul and our life, that Thou didst suffer Thy face to be smitten, Thy head to be crowned with thorns, Thy hands and Thy feet pierced through? Yes, now I would understand and love the sufferings which humble me and purify me, which bring down my proud spirit, and chastise my sensual flesh. May the tide of my life ebb towards my heart, and there concentrate itself, may it be reunited to Thee, my God, in the unity of holy love.

MEDITATION XVII.

Mother of the Saviour, pray for us!

O Mary, thou art the Mother of the Saviour and the Mother of Salvation. God alone is the Father of Salvation, thou, O holy Virgin, art its Mother.

Wherein can we, and ought we, to imitate the Mother of the Saviour? In this, that each soul, in some sense, should be mother of its own salvation. God alone can be the .Father, but the soul is its mother by co-operating with Him. God could create us without ourselves, but He does not save us without ourselves. In saving each soul, God chooses to have a help-mate. This help-mate is the soul herself, with her will, her liberty, her efforts, her labour, and her merits.

Mother of the Saviour, Mother of the salvation of all men, pray for us, that we may learn more and more through thee the necessity of striving, of combating, of working, and of meriting.

We have scarcely emerged from the age when our brethren who separated from the Church taught that man's endeavours, his works and his merits, were nothing, and when by insisting on "God alone," and "Jesus alone," they forgot man, his free-will, and his merits. They forgot the fatal power of sin, as well as the glorious power of man's works, which are wrought in God.

Four errors were interwoven in their dark
doctrine: they undervalued sin as an obstacle
to salvation; they undervalued good works as
a means of salvation; they undervalued reason
and free-will as the agents of each man's salvation; and they caused men to forget the
Mother of the Saviour, the Mother of salvation. They knew not that each soul is the
mother of its own salvation, nor that thou, O
Mother of Christ, art the mother of all salvation.

These deadly doctrines, whose slightest
trail poisons all life, have left some small
trace even among the faithful. Have we not
seen divines in France timid and reserved in
respect of thy worship, O Mary, and at the
same time almost in despair as to the power of
man's works? "Let us seat ourselves in
humility," said they, "in the darkness of this
valley of tears, until the light comes to us
from on high." The sentiment was good, but
they forgot that the light is already come, and
that Christ long ago had said, "Rise up and
walk." Why not then rise up and walk,
when Jesus commands it? Because we forgot
that our free-will must co-operate for our own
salvation, that Mary is the Mother of salvation, and each soul the mother of its own.
These divines who ventured into the dangerous
neighbourhood of Protestants, could not bear
the thought of the Immaculate Conception:
they believed that evil had infected the work
of God to its very centre, to the very soul of
the Mother of God; and that original sin had
corrupted the whole mass, so as to leave in

man, no spark of reason, and no trace of
liberty. They exaggerated predestination to
the destruction of justice, and glorified grace
to the suppression of freedom. They had
too great faith in evil; they gave too many
souls to hell, and their doctrines of despair
only served to multiply the numbers of those
who refused to rise up and walk, because they
knew not the mystery of the Mother of Salvation, nor their duties as children of such a
mother.

In proportion then, O Mary, as Christians
shall know thee better as Mother of Salvation,
and shall understand better the duty of following and imitating thee, and of uniting
themselves to thee, not merely by their love
and their knowledge, but still more by their
acts and their endeavours, is it not clear that
greater and greater numbers will correspond
to the grace of God? Is it not true that the
Christian soul, in which Christ is beginning to
be formed by the Sacraments, will acquire a
mother's heart, with all her anxieties, her
watchfulness, and her courage? Men will
come to understand better one of the meanings
of those wonderful words wherein our Lord
proclaims the law of the last judgment, and
declares that souls will be saved or lost according to their works, or rather according to their
one work—"I was hungry and ye fed me,
thirsty and ye gave me drink, naked and ye
clothed me, sick and ye visited me." What
does this mean? In the sense which we are
now developing it means, as our Lord Himself explains it, that it is Himself whom you,

like a tender mother, have visited, clothed,
and fed, every time that you have exercised a
mother's office in respect of His formation
within the least of souls, within thine own soul,
O Christian.

Yes, this is the law of the last judgment.
It is not enough to say: " A Child is born to
us, who is the Saviour;" it is for you also,
O Christian soul, to cry out with joy, " I am
His Mother.   Henceforth it is my part to
watch and to work for Him ; when He is
hungry, I must feed Him , when He is thirsty,
I must give Him drink ; when He is weak, I
must support Him ; when He is naked, I
must clothe Him."

And what would you be then, O Christian
soul, if you left Him without food when He
was hungry and thirsty, and took no care of
Him when He was weak and naked ?   What
would you be in the order of grace ? Mothers,
I will not say among mankind, but even among
beasts, mothers, by an infallible instinct, immediately assume all the strength, all the
courage, all the patience, all the intelligence
of motherhood ; what are you Christian soul,
child of Mary, if you know not that you also
are mother of the Saviour, if you cannot or will
not, in union with the Blessed Virgin, assume
the strength, the intelligence, the watchfulness of the Mother of salvation in behalf of
Jesus Christ ?

Mary, Mother of the Saviour, pray for us !
drive away sleep, weakness, idleness, and
sloth, from Christian souls, and from the midst

of the Christian nations. Our Saviour is born,
let us rise up and walk; let us watch and work
to bring Him up, and to make Him grow
amongst us; let us know the eternal merit,
and the divine power of works wrought in God
and for God.

O my God, may I never more say unto
Thee, " I am waiting for grace, I am waiting
for faith and for light," for grace is already
given me; I have enough grace, enough faith,
enough light even now to do the will of God:
and if I do this will to-day, I shall have to-
morrow enough grace, and enough light, to do
it to-morrow. Yes, O Lord, in Thy wisdom,
and Thy mercy, Thou givest us day by day
our daily bread, and not a store for years.
The first grace requires a first obedience, and
then comes another grace, which requires a
fresh response of the soul's intelligence and freedom; and he who works with the grace he has
received, and uses the talent which has been
given him, will always receive more. But our
first grace has been long given us, and a thousand
others have followed. I have nothing more to
wait for then, O my God, to enable me to do
the good Thou requirest of me; I have enough,
it is Thou who waitest for me. Wherefore
then, O my soul, does not the world make
progress towards knowledge, justice, life, and
holiness, except because man waits while he
is waited for? In my soul, as well as in the
world, God is always striving to be born, and
to grow; but how often does the divine seed
find the activity, the generosity, and the un-
wearied courage, of the true mother's heart?

O admirable Mother, do thou pray for us; obtain for us fervour, courage, and zeal for God.

———

MEDITATION XVIII.

Mother most powerful, pray for us.

O powerful Virgin pray for us! Obtain a spark of courage for our feeble souls, for our fainting nature. Make us to know thy power, and the power which through thee, in God, every soul and all mankind may obtain.

The principal and proper power of man, is the power of prayer: " Whatsoever ye shall ask in my name," says the Saviour, " ye shall obtain it." These words are addressed to that company of which Mary is Queen. It is fully and absolutely true, without any exception, that whatever the Mother of God and Queen of men asks of God shall be given to her. But you will say, this is a sort of omnipotence; doubtless it is so; the Mother of God is omnipotent; she is omnipotent by grace, as God by nature. This is as it were, an axiom of theology; that which belongs to God by nature, belongs to the Blessed Virgin by grace. The God-Man, as man, has all power in heaven and on earth, as the Gospel says; but Christ and Mary are of one heart and one soul, they are together the heart and the life-spring of the regenerated world, and it is certain that God performs all the wishes of His heart,

according to the text: "When two of you
agree, all that they ask for shall be given
them." How much more shall the Blessed
Virgin, united to Jesus Christ by the most
wonderful union, so as to be but one heart and
one soul with Him, how much more shall she
obtain all that she asks, unconditionally, without any possible exception! Well, we must
say the same of every soul which is united to
this great heart, and which lives by the inspiration of its spirit. Whatever she asks, she
obtains. Has not God said it? "I do the
will of those that fear me." How much more
will He do the will of those that love Him!

Besides this universal power of prayer, given
to those who live in union with the all-powerful Virgin, herself indissolubly united to Jesus
Christ, the first and most important of the
special powers which is granted to the soul,
is the power of overcoming sin. To the powerful Virgin it is given to crush the serpent's
head; to souls who are united to her, it is
given to overcome sin. Now this is what
you, O Christian soul, must believe with an
unshaken faith, with a firm hope. Whatever
may have been the past state of your soul,
its future may be preserved from evil. Say
not that you are engaged in the most fruitless
of all conflicts, and that, for a quarter or
perhaps for half a century, your life has been
like the life of the world, in which day succeeds
the night, and night the day; that grace has
succeeded sin, and sin, in its turn, driven out
grace, and that a fatal vicissitude seems to
bind you by an invisible chain, which is some-

times relaxed, but can never be broken. Say not that you must necessarily die thus, striving in vain to fill the vessel which empties itself, or to place on the holy temple the stone which falls continually just as it reaches the top. Say not that all other graces are given to you, but that perseverance alone is denied to you, and, in consequence, all progress in good, all growth in God, and all hope of eternal life. O Christian soul, who art discouraged by continual falls, rise up; the powerful Virgin can do all. She, who corresponds faithfully to all grace, and has never wasted an opportunity, can change the issue of a combat in which you appear to have been losing ground for a long time. Put forth one more generous effort to unite yourself to the Mother of Salvation, and to become the mother of your own life; you must strive to merit it for yourself; one more generous effort, and you will assuredly come off victorious! You have been living in habitual degradation with your old wounds unhealed, and one fall ever leading to another; you are now to live in glory and triumph, and are to hear the sentence of our Saviour: "To him that overcometh, I will give a new name, and I will give him power over the nations."

What does this mean, O my God, and what is this power over the nations, which Thou dost give to souls that are victorious over sin? It means that he who has overcome evil in himself, begins to overcome it for others, and that he who is united to the King of the nations, and to the mighty Queen who crushes the serpent, becomes one of their ministers for the salvation of mankind, and for the healing of the nations, of whom the Scripture says: "God has made the nations of the earth capable of cure." Such a one works for this end, whether by his labours, or by his example, or by preaching, if he is called to it, or by prayer, which is all-powerful.

And is not this, O powerful Virgin, the most unexpected gift of power which thou bestowest on thy children? To heal the nations, to transform the world! And who tells us that the world can be transformed? Is not the world progressing towards its decrepitude? Is not faith growing weak? Ever since the beginning of the world, has not mankind been like a sinful soul, which relapses after every fresh grace, and whose only answer to every call of God is to fall away? Is not the whole human race perverted by old habits of sin? Have not the accumulated crimes of each generation, added to the sins of their fathers, hastened the world's fall as it grew older? It is this deluge of sin that the soul which has but just conquered herself through Jesus and Mary, would stop and overcome. Yes, say the saints, this is our desire, and if our Mother asks it, we can do it. What Christian would dare deny it? Who shall say that Mary asks these things and that she shall not obtain them? And who shall dare assert that she does not ask them? Those who doubt this know not the all-powerful Virgin, "the Virgin hitherto unknown," as the Venerable Grignon de Montfort has called

her. And this holy man, whose wisdom and
virtue shine forth in these days, after having
been forgotten for nearly a century, adds:
"I wish to show that the divine Mother has
been unknown up to this time, and that this
is one of the reasons why Jesus Christ is not
known as He ought to be. If, then, as is certain, the reign of Jesus Christ does come upon
the earth, it will be but a necessary consequence of the knowledge and of the reign of
the ever-blessed Virgin Mary, who first
brought Him forth into the world, and who,
hereafter, will make Him more known.
Therefore, God wishes that His holy Mother
should be more known, more loved, more
honoured, than she has ever been before.
Mary must be more conspicuous than ever in
mercy, in strength, and in grace, in these
latter times. God wishes to clothe her anew,
and to put her forward as the master-piece of
His hands. He reserves her to form and
educate the great saints who shall live at the
end of the world."

At that time wonderful things shall come
to pass in these low regions, for the Holy
Ghost, finding His beloved Spouse formed in
the souls of men, will descend and abundantly
fill them with His gifts, and particularly with
the gift of wisdom, and will work wonders of
grace. O Christian soul, when shall this time
be?

All should receive this consoling doctrine—
all should encourage this holy hope. God,
since the beginning of the world, and especially since Christ's coming, has ever gratui-

tously poured out upon mankind His prevent-
ing and exciting grace, almost without our
co-operation, as when the grace of baptism
regenerates the unconscious infant—God, if I
may say so, waits for the moment when mankind shall put away childish things, as St. Paul
requires, and shall arrive at the age of clear
discretion and true freedom, and so shall be
able to choose with more prudence between
life or death, and to appropriate more firmly
the gifts of God. Everything is offered, everything is given, but mankind has scarcely understood or used the gift. Jesus Christ is developed in the Church, but He has scarcely come
to manhood among the nations of Christendom.
He has not yet reached that perfect growth
which will be the consummation of the elect;
nor has He yet come to that full age, to that
degree of the mystical growth of His reign
upon the earth, which the Church and every
Christian daily prays for: "Thy kingdom
come, Thy will be done on earth, as in
heaven." A prayer of deepest meaning, which
almost all of us have the misfortune to repeat
every day without attaching the least meaning to it.

In these days, Jesus Christ lives and works
in the Church, as He lived and worked for
thirty years by Mary's side, while He waited
for the time of His miracles and His manifestation.

And for what is He to wait but for that
happy age, when the Holy Spirit shall find
His beloved Spouse, the Virgin, more perfectly
formed in our souls, and shall overshadow them

more fully, and fill them with His gifts? And how is this progress to be made, if not by the efforts of man, to help, to accept, and to retain more faithfully the grace already given, and to merit like the Blessed Virgin, and through her assistance and example, to carry God within him in ever-increasing measure, and to communicate to the world His eternal life?

O my God! I understand why Thy Church, the sole safeguard of progress in the world, witnesses with indifference, sometimes even with fear, the preachers of progress. The reason is, because in reality all these apostles, so far as we have heard them, preach progress, but practice nothing but ruin. Do we not know that the spirit of lying teaches its followers to call day night, and night day, as Holy Scripture says? In this way the decline of this century has been called progress. When we are told of progress, which comes through pride and intoxication of the senses, we may be sure that it is the progress of hell, that is to say, the progress of a retrograde movement towards what is beneath man, instead of towards God. On the contrary, when we see an increase of the virgin virtues of humility, of chastity, of purity, we may then believe in every kind of progress, the progress of justice, the progress of charity, the progress of science, the progress of genius, the progress of freedom, the progress of power, that shall overcome the world, and shall give laws to the nations. Therefore, the Catholic Church, by furthering

with all its strength the idea and the worship
of the Immaculate Mother of God, is the true
furtherer of all progress.   Yes, Lord, I desire
the progress of my soul, and the progress of
the world.   I will devote myself, to this, to
restrain my passions, to repress my pride, to
live in humility and purity.   Will this be too
great a price to pay for wisdom, increase of
virtue, truth, freedom, and life, first for myself,
and then for my fellow-men?

MEDITATION XIX.

Virgin most faithful, pray for us.

Virgin most faithful, to whom the Word
incarnate deigned to submit for thirty years,
and who didst make use of this treasure of all
grace so perfectly and faithfully as to open to
all the elect the well-spring of life, to found
and to enlarge the indivisible heart of the
Church, which is made up of thine immaculate heart, together with that of Jesus,—to
prepare, by the pulsations of this heart, all
mankind to receive the Word, the Blood, and
the Spirit of our Saviour—O Mary, Virgin
most faithful, pray for us, that we too may be
faithful; let our hearts beat in sympathy with
thine, that we may learn to receive with ever
greater faithfulness the gifts of God, and to
make use of them to prepare the way for the
glorious reign of Jesus Christ.

Make us all understand how everything now depends on our faithfulness. God has lent us His talents, it is for us to put them to interest. It is for us to choose which of the servants in the Gospel we will resemble. Will we copy the good and faithful servant who used his one talent so as to gain ten, or the wicked and slothful servant, who buried his talent in the earth, and there left it idle ?

Shall mankind still bury in its bosom the treasure of the Incarnate Word, and leave His Gospel, His cross, His life, and all the virtue of His blood that was shed for us, unfruitful to the end?

St. Gregory the Great has some terrible words on this subject, in a Commentary on the text of the Gospel where the master comes for the third time to visit the barren figtree, and commands his servants to cut it down. "Yes," he says, "the master of the vineyard in our day is come the third time to visit His figtree, He has come three times to call men, to wait for them, to warn them, and to visit them, before the law, under the law, and under grace. He came before the law, because He teaches us by natural reason what each of us owes to His brethren : He came under the law to give us His positive commands ; He comes after the law by grace, to give men the real presence of His divine goodness. And this is why He complains of finding no fruit any of these three years, because so many wicked men are touched neither by the inspiration of the natural law nor by the commands of the written law, nor by the miracle of the Incarnation."

Virgin most faithful, Queen and Mother of mankind, wilt thou suffer us, by our perpetual faithlessness, to become barren figtrees, unimproved by all the gardener's toil? Shall this barrenness be the last state of mankind? Will God be obliged to say to us what the master of the vineyard said to the bad tree: "Cut it down, why cumbereth it the ground?" Or rather, most faithful Virgin, Queen and mistress of mankind, wilt thou not say to God what the gardener said to his master: Lord, have patience yet one year, and I will dig around it, and manure its roots, and perhaps it will bear fruit: if not, then cut it down?

Yes, this is our hope, that the new toils of the gardener may heal our barrenness. Through thee, most faithful Virgin, through a more enlightened knowledge of thee, through imitating thee, through a greater development of thy worship, man may yet become more faithful, and prepare the earth to bring forth the fruits of the kingdom of God. Man may yet put out his talent to interest, and God, who, in St. Gregory's forcible words, waits for mankind, may yet find a harvest upon the earth, when He sends forth His reapers.

What, then, are these new toils of the husbandman for the growth of the divine seed? What is to be this increased faithfulness of man, as steward of the treasure which is placed in his hands? What is it that God waits for?

The treasure, or divine seed, is the Incar-

nate Word ; the labours which He waits for
are those which He commands in His Gospel,
and which He declares will decide the salvation of each soul, and of the world.   He is
hungry, and would be fed; naked, and would
be clothed; sick, and would be visited; but
how can Jesus Christ be sick, and naked, and
hungry, and thirsty ?   I own that unless He
had said so, it would have been incredible,
but He has said : " I was hungry, and thirsty,
sick, and naked ;" and He adds, " every time
ye have done so to the least of these little
ones, ye have done it unto me."

This, then, is what God is waiting for.   Or,
to speak more plainly, Jesus Christ is waiting
in expectation till His mystical body, which is
the Church, and in some sense all mankind,
as St. Thomas Aquinas says—He is waiting
till this mystical body, which, in so many of
its members is hungry, thirsty, naked, sick,
and in prison, shall become the object of a far
greater solicitude to those who have the grace
and the power.   He would have us treat His
mystical body, · as Mary, the faithful Virgin,
treated His Childhood.

Yes, Christ asks to be fed, cured, clothed,
and educated in the persons of the poor, the
sick, the naked, and the ignorant.   He requires us to remove the hindrances to His
growing to perfect manhood.   He asks for
Himself this care and these toils.   And why ?
because this care and these toils develop the
virtues of the faithful Virgin in the soul of
the man who gives himself to them, and in
the souls of those on whom they are exercised.

That is to say, because they prepare the way for the growth of the Word amongst men.

He waits for mankind to bestow a different education on children, on the ignorant and the weak, and a different charity on the poor. He expects that we should see Him in the child we educate, and in the poor whom we relieve.

Virgin most faithful, pray for us, obtain for us the gift of faithfulness. Give us that Mother's heart towards the Infant Jesus, which is the only pledge of true fidelity. Let us be the mother and faithful handmaid of Jesus Christ; let us never more abandon or neglect His childhood, His weakness, His hunger, His thirst, His nakedness, or His poverty.

May we never hereafter neglect the least of these little ones, who are in captivity, either in our own soul, or in other men, where the Son of Man waits for us to release Him, that He may increase and reign.

Yes, Lord, I will make fresh endeavours to till the ground of my own soul, and the whole field of human nature. I could never understand the neglect of mankind for its poor, its sick, its dying, its children; it scandalizes its children, it deceives the dying by concealing their danger; it looks at the poor without understanding them, without seeing God in them. But thanks be to God, this is scarcely true now of Christian countries. Where the Spirit of St. Vincent of Paul has gone forth,— and where has it not ?—those endeavours, which in all ages of the Church had been practised

by the saints, have been redoubled. There is
a greater respect for His Childhood in children,
for His poverty in the poor and sick, arising
around us, and attracting the hearts of men.
These forms of Catholic worship win the nations which have come to maturity, as its
visible splendours win the nations which are
still children. Be brave, then, O Christians, advance with more and more determi-
nation in the worship of the poverty of Jesus,
His childhood, His captivity, His weakness,
and His suffering. This worship will be the
true fertilising of the earth, the tillage which
God will bless, which will deliver the world
from its moral barrenness, and which may
prepare a rich harvest for the last ages of man's
life upon earth.

MEDITATION XX.

Virgin most merciful, pray for us!

Virgin most merciful, pray for us; teach us
by what means thy heavenly likeness may be
multiplied among men; teach us how to hope
that a greater number of souls may attain to
thy virtues; that souls which are better prepared, because they are more like to thee, may
receive more abundantly the Holy Spirit, and
that the Holy Spirit being more worthily received amongst men, the mystical Body of
Jesus Christ may develop with increased

splendour, and may hasten the coming of His kingdom.

For this end, Virgin most merciful, make us understand what mercy is.

Mercy, if we look at the real sense, and at the root of the word, is not only a gentleness which pardons, but also a goodness which communicates itself,—it is one soul going forth to meet another.

Thus, not only does thy merciful soul, O Mary, go forth to meet other souls, but she also communicates and gives herself to all. Mary, as the Church tells us in the office of the Immaculate Conception, gives herself to all, and seeks to fill every thing. And, as the Sun of Justice, Jesus Christ, our God, makes His light shine on the good and on the wicked, so the Blessed Virgin, this unchangeable light, sheds upon all men the rays of her mercy, and shows herself to all full of sweetness and clemency.

That is to say, this perfect Virgin imitates God.

"God exists necessarily," says St. Thomas, "and is therefore necessarily good, and therefore expansive, and therefore He must give Himself to any one who can receive Him." And the foundation of our religion is Jesus who gives Himself to all, who died for all, who came to give all men His blood, His flesh, His soul, His Spirit, His divinity. And now the mystery of the kingdom of God, of the progress of the Church, and of the world, is open to our view.

There is God the Father, the giver of all;

there is Jesus, King of men, also giver of all ;
there is the most holy Virgin, Mother of God,
Queen and Mother of mankind, who receives
and transmits all that is given ; there are the
saints who receive and transmit the waves of
grace; why then does not the light, the life,
the grace, the Spirit of God, come to all, even
to the lowest, even to those whom our Lord
calls the least of the little ones ?

Evidently the cause must be something
which is an obstacle to the coming of the kingdom of God, and to God's being all in all;
the chain of grace must be broken somewhere.
The waves of light, and the torrents of pleasure,
as the Scripture call them, well forth from the
Father, and flow on to the Word, to the Incarnate Word, and from the Word to the
Immaculate Virgin, who receives, gathers up
and passes on the fulness of the gifts. Under-
neath the Virgin, the saints pass on each his
own part of the gift which he receives, but
beneath the saints the confusion begins. There
are found the souls who are called to holiness,
but never reach it; there are found the
guiltiest perhaps of souls, those to whom Jesus
and Mary give much, but who accept little, and
pass on still less; there it is that the chain of
graces is broken; it is there that the sun's
rays are stopped; and why? because these
souls never go forth to meet their fellows;
they are concentrated in themselves, they have
not love enough, they love not with the love
which goes out of itself, and gives itself either
to God to receive His grace, or to their neighbour to pass it on.

In the mystical Body of Christ, these souls are members which stop the blood, veins through which no life runs. This is the mystery of iniquity, the mystery of self-love ; opposed to the love of God, and of mankind. These are the souls of which St. James speaks, who pray selfishly, and only ask for life in order to consume it on their lusts. These are the stewards of whom the Gospel speaks, who sleep, drink, eat, and beat their fellow-servants, while waiting for the return of their master.

And what is probably required by numbers of these souls, to enable them to pass over to the side of the saints, to leap over the wall, to cease to be obstacles, and to become instruments, to pass on the light and the life instead of stopping them ? They require a little more knowledge of the mystery of the Virgin, and a little more faithfulness in her worship. They require to learn from the Mother of mankind how to make their soul expand towards their neighbour.

The prophet Isaias explains all this to us: You who are called by God, who believe yourselves Christians, and perhaps pious and holy ones, listen well to this solemn lesson : "They seek me from day to day, and desire to know my ways, as a nation that hath done justice, and hath not forsaken the judgments of their God : they ask of me the judgment of justice : they are willing to approach God ! Why hast Thou not regarded ?' say they to God: we have humbled ourselves, and Thou hast not taken notice !"......This is the state of these souls, and the inspired text teaches us, that

they are thus barren because they are attached
to themselves, and know not how to give, but
weary themselves in their selfishness. Then
the prophet adds in God's name: " Is not this
rather what I have chosen? loose the bands of
wickedness, undo the bundles that oppress, let
them that are broken go free. Deal thy
bread to the hungry, and bring the needy and
harbourless into thy house: when thou shalt
see one naked, cover him. Then shall thy
light break forth as the morning, and thy
health shall speedily arise, and thy justice
shall go before thy face, and the glory of the
Lord shall gather thee up.

" Thou shalt call, and the Lord shall hear :
thou shalt cry, and He shall say : Here I am.
When thou shalt pour out thy soul to the
hungry, and shalt satisfy the afflicted soul, then
shall thy light rise up in the darkness, and thy
darkness shall be as the noon-day.

" And the Lord will give thee rest continually, and will fill thy soul with brightness,
and deliver thy bones, and thou shalt be like
a watered garden, and like a fountain of water,
whose waters shall not fail."—(Isaias ch. lviii).

If we could but understand these deep
mysteries, O Virgin most merciful, whose soul
condescends to all, and pours itself forth into
all souls! thou who art the noon-day of light,
the living fountain that never faileth, teach
our souls to understand, to feel, and to practise thy virtues, that in God, and through
thee, they may become full of unfailing light.

Shall we never understand that all mankind is one whole, a body in which each

7

member receives and ought also to give?
Life should live and circulate; it comes to
all, he who would stop it loses it. He who
consents to lose it, finds it. Each soul, if it
would live, should pour itself forth into
another soul. But what is this other soul?
Are we speaking of human love and friendship? No. We are speaking of that poor
and hungry soul, that man, whoever he is,
whom Jesus calls the least of these little ones.
We are speaking in every sense of the words,
of feeding the hungry, of helping the weak, of
clothing the naked, of delivering the prisoner.
So that as our Lord says, men have but one
duty, as there is but one rule for the last
judgment—to serve God in the poor, to take
care of Christ in His Childhood and poverty,
in the least of His little ones. O God, shall
we be always without reason or feeling? Shall
we never understand this manifest law of true
religion? How long shall the man who receives from God some gift, whether life, or
strength, or youth, or health, or knowledge, or
faith, or any other gift of grace, or mere silver
and gold;—how long shall he go on fancying
that this gift is to stop in him and be con-
sumed by him? how long shall he refuse to
understand that every gift of God, is a force
which must be passed on, in order to be preserved and multiplied?

How long shall those who have received in
good measure some gifts of God behold without emotion the immense multitude of men
famishing in soul, in mind and in body? How
long shall they forget that in the least of His

little ones the Incarnate Word suffers and endures?

How long shall Christian nations refuse to believe that Christ expects from them a different education for His childhood, a different care for His poverty, whether within themselves, or around them, in those multitudinous races which still sit in the weakness of their world-old poverty, and aged childhood?

When shall we learn that the kingdom of God consists entirely in this point, thus expressed in the sacred text: " Give and take, and justify thy soul?" (Eccl. xiv. 16.) To receive from the Father and from the Incarnate Word, and from the Mother of God, some rays in order to transmit them to the last and least of the poor; to perpetuate in this manner out of disinterestedness and the spirit of sacrifice, the chain of graces and the progress of light; that we may receive from God a double portion of light and grace, again to transmit them from an overflowing and ever more generous heart?

If we would but comprehend these truths, and if we would begin practising them at the easiest end, namely, by a more liberal bestowal of our gold and silver, that we may come by degrees, like Jesus and Mary, to give our sweat and our blood, is it not plain, that, by degrees also, the virtues of the Mother of God would enter into our souls, her likeness be engraved there, that the Spirit of God would pour Itself out on them, that the Word would grow in them, first of all in those who give, and then in those who receive, and that the reign of God would prosper among men ?

O Virgin most merciful, thou seest how hard it is for us to understand these truths, to see them clearly when we get a glimpse of them, and, above all, to practise them; thou knowest the obstacles which hinder the soul from receiving all that God would bestow, and from passing on all that it has received; pray then, that by fresh endeavours we may come nearer to this light and this power, pray that we may be able to approach nearer to thee, the pure well-spring of the light and the power which God grants to men. Pray that we may come to know the obstacle which hinders our soul from receiving all that God would give it, and from passing on the little which it has received.

MEDITATION XXI.

Mother of mercy, pray for us !

Mother of mercy, pray for us ! Obtain for us the virtue of mercy, or tenderness of heart. Only the pure heart is merciful. Without thy immaculate heart, there would be no mercy in the world. Obtain for us that purity of heart, whose fruit is compassionate love.

Mother of mercy, when thou holdest in thine arms the divine child who carries the world surmounted with His cross, thou be-

holdest this world brimful of sorrows, and
thou sayest, Behold my Son who shall wipe
away the tears from every eye.

Jesus also beholds this globe, and sees the
people sitting in darkness, and the shadow of
death, beaten down, trodden underfoot, and
scattered like sheep without a shepherd. He
beholds all these sorrows at one glance, and
He says, "I will give my life for them."
And the Mother of mercy says, "I will give
my Son for them." "I am come," says our
Saviour, "to cast fire on the earth, and how
do I long for its kindling." What is this fire,
O Jesus, but that which Catholic piety represents in pictures, where we see the heart of
Mary pierced with a sword, coupled with the
Heart of Jesus crowned with thorns, with
flames issuing from both? These flames are
the flames of love, they are the flames of compassion that has become love, even to the
desire of martyrdom, at the sight of the
miseries of the world.

And we, shall we never have a single spark
of this fire? Shall no other hearts but those
two ever know the hearty, intelligent, active,
efficacious, fervent pity, the heavenly mercy,
which involves forgetfulness of self, and de-
voted itself even to death and martyrdom?
Shall not this fire spread its consolations over
the earth, O Mary, Mother of mercy, through
the growth of the knowledge and the imitation
of thee?

O Mary, let our eyes see, let our minds
know, let our hearts feel this glance of Jesus'
eye upon the world. Help us to keep our

thoughts fixed on this globe surmounted by
the cross which is borne by the Infant Jesus
in the arms of His Mother. Instead of limit-
ing our view within the sphere of our own
interest, of our own persons, teach us to extend it to the whole world. Is this world, O
men, too large for your hearts, while Jesus
your brother, Himself a man, supports it in
one hand ? This world, which your brethren
of the race of Adam, the heroes of the earth,
have found too small for their glory ? At this
very time science is about to lay down electric
lines by which all parts of the world will be
connected together, and by means of which
two men from one pole to the other will speak
to each other, as if they were joining hands !
And think you, that while these inferior forces,
latent in the metal which transmits them,
thus encircle the whole world, the spiritual
force latent in, and emanating from, the human
soul shall be less extensive and ever unable to
encircle the world ?

There is a nation which always keeps its
eyes on all parts of the globe. They study
and consider it ; they seek for all that is to be
had in it, and for the shortest roads by which
to bring all things into their possession. And
when a fresh portion has been discovered,
which contains some hidden mine of wealth,
of whatever kind it may be, that portion is
immediately drained to swell the treasure of
the rich metropolis, to which their hearts are
attached. O my God, shall there not also be
another kind of investigators, whether in the
midst of this very nation or elsewhere, who

shall know how to study and consider the
world, who shall know what service they have
to render to it; and if possible, what are the
necessities of each nation, of each individual,
and what ways and means will bring to all
true light and life?

O Mother of Mercy, the world is now spread
out before me; guide me, and show me what
I ought to see there; teach me, I pray thee,
how to look upon the world.

And, first of all, I see what the Saviour
saw, men seated in darkness and the shadow
of death. This darkness covers three quarters
of the earth; Christians form but the fifth
part of the whole population of the world.
And yet those nations that are Christians are
the masters of the world. Their science, their
arts, the wonders of their discoveries, the order
of their undertakings, the vigour of their asso-
ciations, give them power to change the face
of the earth whenever they choose. They have
but to wish it. In the meanwhile, the rest of
mankind rots away in nameless vices, in sorrow, degradation, want, frightful miseries, in
all the inexpressible horrors of savage and
barbarous life. The systematic murder of
infants, the slavery of women, universal and
unrestrained licentiousness, intemperance that
undermines the constitution of races, a deadly
indolence, brute passions of destruction, the
union of rage and hunger which drives man to
eat man's flesh, such are the most striking
points in the picture.

When I turn my eyes towards Christian
nations, my first surprise is to see how they

witness the frightful spectacle of the suffering
world without any deep emotion, and without
seeking, as Scripture says, to order the whole
world in justice and equity. But this is only
because they are far from enjoying the full
light of God.

The light comes down from heaven, but
where are they who receive it? The little
they receive from without makes them the
masters and guides of mankind, but what blind
guides! They use their light for their bodily
pleasure, for ruling over nature, for extending
the dominion of physical science, and of the
arts which fashion matter; their social virtues
are earthly, and have no reference to eternal
life; and the supernatural light of Jesus Christ,
that eternal light which was to heal our fallen
nature, and to raise it on high, though it has
healed some wounds, has not greatly elevated
the whole mass, which is still stubborn against
its influences.

Even of those who believe themselves to be
Thine, O Christ, every one employs what little
light and strength he has chiefly for his own
good; none is without an eye to self in serving Thee; none looks beyond his own narrow
circle; none beholds the world and its misery,
or Thy cross. The virtue of mercy, of loving
pity, never flames up in these straitened
hearts; their eyes are tearless when they behold
the sorrows of soul and body that surround
them. Far from wishing through love of man,
and through love of Thee, to make the whole
world serve Thee, scarce any one thinks of con-

verting his own town or his own house to Thy
service.

Instead of enquiring all over the world what
each nation needs, they take no trouble to heal
the sorrows which force themselves on their
notice; they forget how the ancient law said,
" thou shalt not permit, O Israel, a single in-
digent person among thy tribes;" or if they
think of it, they believe that this law was for
the Jews, and not for Christians.

This coldness of heart, which refuses to be
kindled by the flames which proceed from the
hearts of Jesus and Mary, is the reason of the
slow progress of the world.   O Mother of
Mercy, when wilt thou warm these hearts
which thou wouldst kindle, but which never
burn, these hearts nearest to thine after those
of the saints, yet perhaps most guilty of all,
because they hinder the progress of life, and
divide the bounteous heaven from the craving
earth ?

To my eyes, the world presents but these
two features : the rest is immaterial : there is
the mass of mankind sunk in darkness, and in
the midst of this mass there is Christendom,
only half accepting the light that shines upon
it.   When the light shall kindle into a flame,
as in the hearts of Jesus and Mary, the fire
which Jesus Christ came to cast upon the
earth, shall enfold the whole earth in a moment.

Mother of Mercy, grant me a new heart.
If I cannot renew the world, I will try to renew myself.   Surely, the fire will burn within

me, if with Jesus and thee I often turn mine
eyes on mankind, on this globe surmounted by
the cross.

When I pray, it shall be in the presence of
Jesus and of His Mother, and of this globe
which they carry.

I am determined that no human thing shall
henceforth be without interest for me, for I
know that there is a certain historical science
necessary for the Christian; the science which
takes cognisance of the present state of the
world. I bless God that this science is already
brought down to the level of the merest pea-
sant by the Society for the Propagation of the
Faith. I will study it, that I may teach it;
I will learn it, that I may transmit it, and make
my children learn the science of human nature
suffering beneath our eyes, rather than teach
them the classics of antiquity.

With all my heart, and all my strength, I
will propagate mercy, and daily will I call
upon thy name, O Mother of Mercy. I will
try to make it renowned; I will keep my heart
pure, that the fire may kindle there, for the
least spark of the fires of earth, quenches all
traces of the heavenly fire.

I will try to understand how thy heart, if
it had been for a moment sullied with concupiscence, could never be in union with that of
Jesus, the well-spring of the heavenly fire
which is to cleanse the world, and which Jesus
wishes to see kindled.

I will enter, also, with all my heart, into
the spirit of St. Vincent of Paul, which leads

men back to faith through the paths of compassion.

I will never forget the striking lesson of St.
Vincent's life, how he was tempted to infi-
delity for three years, and overcame the temptation by devoting himself to the poor, thus
regaining a lively faith through practising
that compassion of heart, that sympathy with
the poor, that loving mercy which constitutes
his distinctive spirit. In the presence of this
model, still so near to us, still as it were living
amongst us, I would ask my brethren what is
the use of the days of our life, except to do
some good? What is the use of power and
riches, if not to open the channels of truth and
mercy to the world?

I will try to understand the insensibility,
malice, and stupidity, of habitually beholding
all this darkness and sorrow without taking
any decided and bold steps in behalf of justice
and truth. To see Jesus Christ, and the saints
and the apostles, and the servants of God carrying their cross, and going forth alone to fight
against evil, and to conquer the world to God,
without being drawn on to follow them.

MEDITATION XXII.

Virgin most prudent, pray for us

Virgin most prudent, pray for us, and obtain for us that prudence which perceives the obstacle and avoids it.

The obstacle of the soul, thou, O Virgin most prudent, hast always avoided. Never didst thou allow it to arise in thee, never was there the least hindrance to the entrance of God's light in thee, nor to the transmission of His light to the world; for thou receivedst God Himself: thou didst conceive the very God in thy heart, in thy mind, and in thy body, and thou didst transmit to the world the Incarnate Light.

If the science of the soul was known, men would know what is the obstacle of all souls, and how each soul bears it within her, except the immaculate soul of the Virgin most prudent. Then would they know that conformity with this model is necessary in order to overcome the obstacle to all progress.

Let us try to understand something on this point.

St. Bernardine of Sienna compares thy immaculate heart, O Virgin most prudent, "to the focus of a burning lens, which concentrates from all sides the rays of the sun; the focus collects them, begets the fire, and enkindles everything that comes near to it." No words can give a better idea of the immaculate soul of Mary, without spot or obstacle, conceiving God, imparting God, and fruitful through her virginity.

For if we enquire what constitutes the power of these wonderful mirrors which concentrate the sun within themselves, which contain and send forth its heat, we shall find that it is their collecting together in one focus, in one single centre, all the rays of the sun which fall upon them. Other mirrors also receive the same rays, but they have not the power to concentrate them ; they have no focus, no centre, no single spot to attract them to.

Thus it is that thy prudence, O Mary, which transfigures thy soul into light, consists in reducing into unity and simplicity all the rays of the life which God gives, like the heavenly Jerusalem, of which thou art the Queen and centre, and which is " built as a city, which is compact together."

I am not surprised at the sovereign importance of this simplicity and this unity in the life of the soul, for it is the mark whereby Jesus Christ Himself distinguishes between good and evil, between the life and death of the soul. ." If thy eye be single, thy whole body will be lightsome ; but if it be evil, thy body also will be darksome." (Luke xi. 34.)

These mysterious words show us the law of the human heart, and teach us that it needs only to be simple and at unity in itself in order to possess the light and to dispense it ; while on the contrary, the mere absence of simplicity is enough to make it evil, and incapable of producing anything but darkness.

But what is it that causes our heart to lose its simplicity ?

Listen to the lessons of the masters of the spiritual life. " Woe to the double heart !" says Scripture. The Holy Ghost tells us of a certain doubleness of soul, and the most learned doctors point out to us how it is a necessary consequence of sin. There are in the soul, say they, diverse forces, and amongst these there are two principal ones ; the active force, which understands and judges, and ought to govern ; and the passive force, that of desire, which ought to be governed ; and these forces ought to form but one.

There is, in a manner, a male and female element in the soul ; an Adam and an Eve ; and as it is said that the man and wife are two in one, so the two faculties in the same soul should be two in one.

The soul should be simple, that is, its forces should live in unity, that all the gifts and all the rays of life may be concentrated in this single focus. But is it so ? No. All souls have lost their union, all are at variance with themselves. In all, the passive desire is in schism with the active understanding and judgment. The passive part separates itself from, and often divides, the active powers, enlisting the judgment, without enlisting the understanding. It leaves the reason alone, and drags down the desires and the will to its own abyss. But can we think that the lower part of the soul, the desire, could ever have shaken off the yoke of the higher part, if this had remained faithful ? No, its union was in God, and the forces

of the soul can only be at discord with themselves, by abandoning God. The lower part
of the soul abandons God through sensuality, the higher part through pride. One
grovels in lust, the other soars with presump-
tion. Neither of the two remains in that
central place where the soul can receive God.
The true centre of the soul becomes empty,
and in place of this one centre the soul assumes that double heart which the Gospel
curses, that evil and double eye which fills the
whole soul with darkness.

The true centre of the soul is empty, and
instead of this simple centre, the soul clusters
around two points which divide life between.
them. In one she gathers up the fire which
consumes her, because it is neither chaste nor
luminous; in the other she fancies she stores
up light, but she only stores up a pale reflec-
tion of it, enough to feed pride and error. Then
follows the fearful marriage of the murky and
evil fire with this pale light, the union of
pride and of sensuality, which can produce
nothing but darkness and sin.

These two centres are called by theologians
the concupiscence, the cause and consequence
of sin.

All errors, all sorrows, all evil flow from
this source; it is the true obstacle of the
soul.

This is the teaching of our doctors, derived
from Holy Scripture.

Now we can see, O prudent Virgin, what
thy soul is, and what ours is. Now we
understand how impossible it is that the soul

of the pure Virgin, Mother of God, can have been for an instant divided and decomposed into two centres, so as to change the divine life into pride and sensuality. A single instant of this fearful schism is the loss of true virginity. If original sin, or even concupiscence, had ever been in Mary, if she had not been ever immaculate, her soul was not virginal, her innocence was but mended and patched like ours. But she is in reality the one true Virgin, and never was there in her the slightest trace of sin or concupiscence.

As to ourselves, let us well understand the state of our interior life. Not one of our souls is absolutely single, nor absolutely virginal. Every soul bears within herself the springs of pride and of sensuality, more or less developed, more or less distant from their centre. In all the matter of sin is continually being reproduced, and gains activity day by day through the mere influence of life.

What, then, is the remedy of the soul? It is to fight and to struggle continually that she may return to simplicity, wherein lies her perfection, or at least that she may approach it; and this would be, O Virgin most prudent, to make our souls conformable to thine, to return to God and to thee, to come to God through thee.

The masters of the spiritual life, and especially St. Augustine, say that we have Adam and Eve within us, that one is for us the spring of pride, and the other of sensuality. Why should we not also say that we have within us, in the innermost part of our being, in the sanctuary, as it were, the new Eve and the new Adam, that is to say, thyself and thy Son in one? And certainly it must be so in Christians who receive the body of Jesus, His soul and divinity.

But these two divine guests pass quickly through the lower powers and the exterior circles of the soul, in an instant they are in the centre, where the soul ought to concentrate her powers; they enter there to attract us and to bring back to their centre the two forces purified, the one by humility, the other by chastity.

This is truly the mystery of the progress of souls.

O Mary, pray for us! That the mystery of the progress of souls by their union with thee, and with thy Son Jesus Christ, that the means of returning to simplicity, which is all-powerful, to virginity, which is fruitful, by humility and by chastity, may be better known among men, and that the immeasurable advantages which this return would bestow on each individual soul and on the whole world, may become evident to the eyes of all.

MEDITATION XXIII.

The mystery of the progress of souls is not
yet sufficiently known. The mystery of the
gate of heaven is not yet sufficiently unveiled
in the sight of Christians, even in that of
learned and pious Christians. This is, at
least, the opinion of two authors, who are
alike eminent for their talents and holiness.

We will quote from each successively.

The venerable Grignon de Montfort thus
speaks of the means of attaining true devotion
to the Blessed Virgin, and a faithful imitation
of her, in order that we may dwell in God
through her:

"The practice which I seek to discover is
one of those secrets of grace which are unknown to the greatest number of Christians,
even to the devout, and which are practised
and appreciated by a still smaller number."

And in describing the practice, he first of all
lays down the necessity of fighting against and
extinguishing the springs of concupiscence, the
evil root by which our best actions are ordina-
rily infected and corrupted. "Even when
God pours out the sweet wine of His love, the
heavenly dew of His grace, into the vessel of
our soul foul with original and actual sin, His
gifts are usually poisoned and defiled by the
evil leaven and the root of bitterness which

sin has left in us; all our actions, even those of the highest virtue, are affected by it."

This it is from which we have to free ourselves; and how is it to be done? This root is our life; it is the life of our soul, such as we make it. The secret, continues Grignon, of the true supernatural life, of the life which God wishes to impart to us, is *death to ourselves*, that fruitful and useful death which St. Paul means when he says "I die daily," that death which our Lord enjoins, when He tells us to deny ourselves, to hate our own life. "He who seeketh life shall lose it, and he who consents to lose it, shall find it." (Luke xvii. 33.)

Is it not clear? In order to find this true and perfect life which God desires to infuse into the centre of our souls, which He created to dwell in the centre to which the Incarnate Word is evermore calling us, while the pride of Adam and the sensuality of Eve, the two-fold force of pride and concupiscence, are evermore tempting us away from it;—in order to find this true life, we must renounce the double-hearted life of pride and sensuality; we must die to the life which we know, to find the life we know not. But how are we so to die? What is the secret of this art? Grignon de Montfort explains it.

"To pass from one life to another, or to die requires a starting point; we must have, as it were, a foot-hold in the second, to be able to quit the first. Here then is the well-spring of thy new life; it is the Blessed Virgin in the centre of thy soul, in that centre from which

thou absentest thyself. Thou abidest and
livest in those evil vortices, far from the virginal point in the midst, where God would
have His dwelling-place in thee; enter into
thyself again, come into the midst of thy soul,
by recollection and self-denial. Yield to the
inner working of God, by the intercession of
His holy Mother, and this working will draw
the vortices of the soul towards the centre,
and will purify them by drawing them together,
and will draw them together by purifying
them, and thus from day to day, will renew
thy soul in simplicity, in proportion as, like
St. Paul, thou diest daily."

But once more; what is the secret of this
death? What must we do, thus to die?

"It consists," says Montfort, "in giving
ourselves wholly to the Blessed Virgin, so as
to be wholly Christ's through her; we must
give her our body, with all its senses and
members, our soul with all its powers, our
worldly goods, present and to come, our
spiritual goods, that is our merits, our virtues,
and our good works, past, present, and to
come, without the least reservation, and for
eternity.

"This is voluntary consecration and self-
sacrifice to Christ, through the Blessed Virgin,
by an act, which is a perfect renewal of our
baptismal vow. Now baptism, says St. Paul,
buries us with Christ in death. Complete
self-denial is the voluntary death which God
demands, and of which Jesus has said, 'Unless
a man denies himself and carries his cross, he
cannot be my disciple;' and again, 'Unless a

man forsakes all he has, he cannot be my disciple;' and again, 'A grain of wheat cast into the earth, unless it die, remains alone, but if it dies, it bears much fruit, and becomes an ear.'"

So the grand secret of passing to another life, by that recollection in which God communicates Himself to the soul, is to give ourselves to Christ who is in the midst of us, through the Virgin who is at the centre of our souls.

But these same things may be otherwise illustrated. Bossuet speaks of the secret way that leads to the gate of heaven, that is to thee, O holy Virgin, and calls it a "gate which, though open to the saints since the first ages of the Church, is still perhaps insufficiently understood by the learned;" and he prays God, "that we may all become like little children, as Christ commands, and so may enter this gate, that we may be able to point it out to others more surely and more efficaciously."

And what is this gate? or rather, how do we approach it? For every Christian knows who the gate of heaven is. It is the Virgin, Mother of God. But by what act do we approach her? By true simplicity, says Bossuet, by self-denial. "True simplicity," says he, "causes us to live in continual death, and perfect detachment; it can only be obtained by a perfect purity of heart, by a true mortification and contempt of self. He who shrinks from suffering and humiliation, and from dying to self, shall never enter there:

this is why there are so few who travel far that road, because scarcely any one will go out of himself, for want of which we lose immensely, and deprive ourselves of unimaginable good."

For want of the will to abandon ourselves, we remain in the double vortex of concupiscence, in the pride of Adam, and the false desires of Eve, and never reach the centre, the unity, the simplicity where the Virgin is found, in whom God dwells.

Bossuet continues: "Teach me to perform this act, O my God, this act so vast, yet so simple, which makes over to Thee all that I am, which unites me to all that Thou art. O Jesus, I lie at Thy feet, let me find this one thing necessary. Thou already knowest, O Christian soul, Jesus whispers to thy heart, that this is the true act of self-denial, for it makes over the whole man to God, his soul, his body, his feelings, his desires, all his limbs, all his veins with all the blood in them, all is made over to Thee, O Jesus, do with it whatever Thou wilt."

Can we believe that the fervent prayer of a soul which thus gives itself wholly to God with full freedom, which offers itself and all it has to God through Christ, to Christ through His Mother,—can we believe that a prayer like this will be in vain, that an offering like this will be despised? Who is it moves us to pray, but God? Who gives Himself first, if it be not the incarnate God, God carried in His Mother's arms, and coming into the midst of the world, and into the midst of the soul, where, for so many days, years and ages, He waits patiently for each soul, and for the whole world ?

Here we have a secret, which has ever been too closely kept, though the Church has never ceased to proclaim it; a specific to enable us to pass from earth to heaven, from our evil and divided life, to a holy and simple life. Here we have the means of removing the obstacle, of conquering our double heart, of reuniting our forces which the perversity of our pride and sensuality had kept apart, and had separated from God. This great act re-places us in the sanctuary where the bright-ness of God's presence shines as in a burning glass, to kindle the flames of knowledge and holiness, that they may spread through the world from the focus of the soul, that has thus become Mother of God.

And what is this act, but perfect love, which, as St. John says, casts out fear?

All obstacles disappear before this act, which includes as its consequences the whole force of contrition, and of the sacrament of pen-ance, the desire of which it implies.

This is the mystery of the soul's progress.

O that we might know that an ever in-creasing number of souls would enter on this road of progress, and would practise this law of life. Perhaps, O holy Virgin, Gate of heaven, if our understanding knew it better, our will would submit to it more easily. Perhaps if we knew what Christian death is, and what is the fruit of complete self-abnegation in thee and in Christ, if we knew that light, joy, peace, increase of life, and all the gifts of the Holy Ghost, are its fruits, if we knew that this self-denial is to lose misery and to gain the infinite, if we could look into the depths of the mystery, and there see the necessary steps of the progress of life, the wonderful approach of the soul to God, and the change from temporal to eternal life; if we knew that the deepest mysteries of wisdom and knowledge are hidden like treasures in the practice of this holy law; if we knew how short is this path from earth to heaven, how near in this direction heaven is to earth, how its sweet influences secretly embrace the earth, even in this life, for all those who seek them through thee, O Gate of heaven; then I say, perhaps more men would turn in this direction, would draw heaven down, and would hasten the coming of the kingdom of God, which is the doing of God's will on earth as it is done in heaven.

MEDITATION XXIV.

Mary our Mother, pray for us.

Mary our Mother, Mother of the elect, and Mother of mankind, pray that we may penetrate deeper and deeper into the mystery of this maternity. Show us how thou hast brought us forth to life, and how we may deserve to be called and to be thy children.

In the order of redemption there are in God two degrees of paternity ; that by which He causes His only Son, the God-Man, to be born of the Virgin, and that by which He adopts mankind in Christ, to be brethren and co-heirs of Jesus.   We find the same degrees of maternity in the Blessed Virgin ; she also is by nature, true Mother of the only Son of God, the God-Man, and besides, she is Mother by adoption of all mankind, and especially of all the elect.

How and when did the Virgin Mary become Mother of Christ? It was when the Angel saluted her, and said : " Blessed is the fruit of thy womb."   At that instant, the only Son of God, was conceived in her, by the Holy Ghost.   Let us never be tired of repeating that it was her absolutely stainless purity, which was, on the human side, the principle of the Incarnation.   It was, says St. Chrysostom, because the Virgin was chaste in a degree far above human nature that she conceived in her womb the Lord Jesus Christ.   There is a mutual relation between her divine maternity and her immaculate purity.

And when and how did Mary become our Mother ?   Mary brought forth all her adopted children in the midst of the sorrows of Calvary, when Jesus said to her from His cross, " Woman behold thy Son," and to St. John, " Behold thy Mother."   All the Fathers of the Church acknowledge that these words were addressed through St. John to all the elect: and many theologians affirm that the cry, " Woman, behold thy Son," was the creative

8

word through which all the elect were born of
Mary to God, through adoption, but through
a real and efficacious adoption.   St. Peter
Damian says, that it was as almighty in its
working as the word which consecrates the
bread and wine, and makes them the body and
blood of Jesus.

Mankind, the offspring of the ground, were
the bread and the wine ; by the words, " Behold thy Son," Jesus consecrates them, and
transforms this worthless bread and wine into
His own brethren, and true children of Mary.
Or rather, He makes them into His own mystical body and blood, for as Origen well re-
marks, " Jesus said not, ' this is also thy son,'
but ' this is thy Son :' and He meant, ' this
man, this adopted son, is the same Jesus whom
thou didst bring forth.' " For the elect of
God should be able to say with St. Paul :
" It is no longer I that live, but Jesus Christ
who liveth in me." For Jesus has made us
members of His own body, and sharers in His
divine nature, by collecting us all into a single
body, which is His.

At that solemn moment mankind was consecrated, and the sons of Adam, the offspring
of the ground, became children of God.   At
that moment, the author of the new creation
blessed mankind, created anew in Jesus Christ,
and in Mary, the second Eve, and said to them :
" Increase and multiply."   At that moment,
the supernatural and more than creative work,
which not only renews, but also raises the
creature from the natural to the supernatural
order, which makes nature transcend itself,

and translates it into God's infinity—at that
moment, the eternal work, the eternal sacrifice, of which the daily sacrifice of the altar is
the continuation, was accomplished.

Of all epochs this was the most solemn.

At that moment God gave His only Son for
the salvation of the world; at that hour the
word was fulfilled, " God so loved the world,
that He gave His only Son." At that hour
the Virgin, freely participating in the sacrifice,
offered up more than her own life, and the
Fathers have applied to her that which Jesus
said of God: " She so loved the world that
she gave her only Son." At that hour Mary,
united to Jesus the High Priest, shared His
priesthood, and accepted and offered up her
sorrows. And these sorrows are the pains of
our birth. " According to St. Bernardine of
Sienna," says a learned author, " it is certain
that Mary, by her loving co-operation with the
mystery of the Redemption, truly brought us
forth to the light of grace on Calvary; and
that in the order of salvation, the sorrows of
Mary, in conjunction with the love of the
Eternal Father and the Passion of His Son,
have given birth to all of us, so that in those
precious moments Mary became in the fullest
sense our Mother, by the immensity of her
love, and the generosity of her martyrdom.

" At that moment the Virgin conceived for
the second time, by the power of the word of
God, when Jesus pronounced those mysterious
words: ' Woman, behold thy Son.' Mary
then felt her bowels yearn, and her heart ex-

pand towards the Church, with all the tenderness of a Mother's love."

And as, for the incarnation of Christ, God required the consent of human nature in the person of Mary, so also for this second birth of the Word in His elect God again required her full consent. She is the Mother of the elect, the Mother of mankind, for she willingly bore all the pain of this agonizing birth; she had to sacrifice her only Son, that He might be no longer her only one, and that His word might be fulfilled: "Unless the grain of corn is cast into the earth, and dies, it remains alone; but if it dies, it bears much fruit." By freely and fully accepting death, for her Son and herself,—a sacrifice, which, after that of Christ, is the most wonderful that a human soul ever made—she deserved to become the multiplier of the corn, and to realize the word of the prophet: "Thy womb is a heap of corn."

As for St. John, the representative of all these new children, he was the first to enter on this inheritance, says St. Cyril, and to become son of God and of Mary, through his virginity, and through his remaining close to the cross. Virginity watching the cross and dying on the cross, or sacrifice, is the cause of men becoming children of God.

When will mankind and Christians come to understand the supernatural fecundity of a sacrifice? When shall we see in sacrifice, and in the cross, which is its Christian sign,—I do not mean in the bleeding victim, which is the form of sacrifice in this valley of tears, but in the pure idea of sacrifice—the supreme and universal law of life, or rather the pulsation and growth of life in God? As on a spring morning we may see the plants growing beneath our eyes, by the electrical influence from above: as we see their delicate veins alternately expanding and contracting with the pulsation of the spirit of nature which develops them, and as these two movements are as necessary to their growth as the two movements of our heart to our life; as it is true that nothing can be increased without being first contracted, nothing raised without being first brought low, and that no one, as our Saviour says, can find life without first consenting to lose it,—as it is true that we can only enter into God's infinity by going out of ourselves, and annihilating ourselves in His presence ;—as this great law applies not only to the life and growth of bodies, not only to the life and growth of souls, but to the life of the understanding and thought, let us hope that some day, and that soon, the idea of sacrifice may penetrate the mind of man, through Mary our Mother standing in the presence of Jesus on the cross, and open new realms to science, and to the soul, heart, and courage of man a new era of self-immolation.

The imitation of Mary is the necessary preliminary of the imitation of Jesus, and this will be its triumph. When the knowledge of thee, O Mother of mankind, and the imitation of thee, come to abound in the Church, they will cause virginity and watching by the cross

to abound amongst men, and will bind them
faster to thee.   And by these two things,
which are at bottom but one, we shall merit
to have thee more and more for our Mother,
and Jesus for our Brother.   United to thee
upon Calvary we shall consent more easily to
death.   Knowing what death is, we shall
escape the slavery which St. Paul speaks of
under which the fear of death holds us during
our life.   We shall be free.   Instead of trem-
bling and crouching for fear, we shall stand
upright, we shall hold up our heads towards
heaven, and shall rejoice in a sacrifice which
glorifies God and promotes the unity of mankind. We shall be brethren in thee, O Mother,
and in Jesus our uncreated Brother ; we shall
be members of one body, and by this sacrifice
we shall unite ourselves in one bread and in
one wine, like grains of corn ground together,
or grapes trodden together in the wine-press.
This bread and wine shall be consecrated into
the holy bread and new wine of the kingdom
of God, where we shall learn that life is, on
man's side, a continual offering, a perpetual
sacrifice of self, answered on God's side by a
torrent of eternal glory.

MEDITATION XXV.

Health of the weak, pray for us!

Teach us, then, O Mary, what is that ineffable good which we lose when we refuse to come to thee, by complete self-abnegation; and what are the treasures of life, of joy, of light, of happiness, which we might expect even in this life, if we died to ourselves, and gave ourselves to thee, and found thee, O gate of heaven.

And first, to begin with the smallest things; what corporal blessings might we not obtain in thy service, O health of the weak.

The principal prayer which the Church offers to God, through the Virgin, and which we may call the prayer of the Virgin is, "Grant, O God, to us Thy servants, the grace of health in mind and body, and by the glorious intercession of the Blessed Mary, ever Virgin, deliver us from present sadness and grant us eternal joy."

If we but understood this prayer, and knew what is the health that God gives! But no, we neglect our bodies, as we do all the rest. We have not sufficient fortitude to preserve our bodies, which yet we prize so highly. We are enslaved to the vices which destroy them. We do not die, but kill ourselves. We waste our life, our strength, and our beauty, and bequeath an impaired constitution to our children. Our present sin inflicts numberless

wounds on our body. Our passions visibly
degrade it, and yet men of science refuse
to acknowledge the cause of the evil. They
attribute our infirmities and illnesses to all
causes but the first and chief, and they seek
the remedy anywhere except in the true well-
spring of life.

Will the time never come, O Health of the
weak, when the sick shall have recourse through
thee to the·fountain of life, and when those
who are·strong shall commit their strength to
thee, that thou mayest guard it and renew it
at its fountain-head? What do our teachers
tell us of this secret of the worship of Mary, this
touching and efficacious practice of giving ourselves entirely to Mary? Give, they say, to
her who is the health of the weak, thy body,
with all its senses and its members. Bossuet
says of the act which regenerates the whole
man, that it "gives up to God the whole man,
soul and body, thoughts, sentiments, desires,
all his limbs, all his veins, with all the blood
which they contain, all his nerves to their
smallest ramifications, all his bones, and the
very marrow in the midst of them."

But if this act so fully offers the whole
body to God, can we suppose that God will
refuse to bless it, and to renew it in the first
principles of its life?

Let those who are sick and infirm try with
full faith to offer their body to God through
Mary, by reciting the prayer of the Virgin,
let them offer their body without reserve,
either for life or death, for suffering or for
health; let them offer it entirely, and in de-

tail as minute as Bossuet describes; let them somehow concentrate by some strong effort of prayer all these details of their body into its centre, which is the heart, and then offer to God for His blessing, and for the inspiration of His Holy Spirit, their natural in union with their spiritual heart. Let them seek in a burst of enthusiasm to unite for an instant their body and their soul with God; let them attempt to make this offering during their morning sacrifice; it is not too much to declare that a number of sick persons, whom nothing else would cure, will find their health in thus offering their whole body to God, through her who is the Health of the weak.

Not to speak of the sudden and miraculous cures which certainly occur from time to time, when will our would-be men of science begin to reckon the soul among the forces which act upon the body? When will they come to know that if the soul, when separated from God by sin, is a spent force, a force cut off from the well-spring of its power; when united to God it becomes on the contrary a mighty stream, a river of life, which penetrates the whole body, even to the marrow of the bones? You see full well that if we wish to overcome the inertia of matter, space or distance, the forces which we must use are not solid matter, like iron or brass, but heat and electricity, and yet you cannot understand that to maintain the life of the living body, the principal force is God, is prayer, is the soul.

If this is the case in the purely natural order of bodily forces, how will it be with the

Christian, nourished with the Sacraments of
God? with the Christian to whom thou comest,
O Mary, when Christ gives to our bodies His
Flesh, His Blood, and His Divinity?   Thou
didst give this life-giving flesh to the Incarnate Word, and therefore thou art the health
of the sick.   The last prayer of the priest,
before he communicates at Mass, is: "Let
not the participation of Thy Body, O Lord
Jesus Christ, which I, unworthy, presume to
receive, turn to my judgment and condemna-
tion; but through Thy goodness may it be
to me a safeguard and remedy, both of soul
and body."

Believers may ask why this life-giving Flesh
taken and eaten, does not oftener heal the
body as well as the soul;—is it not because
man too seldom answers the two questions
which Christ asks of those whom He would
heal: "Canst thou believe?" and "Wilt thou
be healed?"   Believers in the real Presence
will understand how, if faith was more lively,
the Flesh of Christ would much oftener work
out the commission of Jesus to His disciples;
"Go heal the sick, and raise the dead to
life."

If we but knew what an Almighty helper,
that man bears within him, who eats the Flesh
of Christ, and drinks that immaculate and life-
giving Blood, which is thine, O Mary, Mother
of God, as well as Christ's; if we but knew
the mystery of regeneration, the bodily resurrection which is wrought in this man, by the
Virgin who conceives God, and by God conceived in Mary, and dwelling in the centre of

the man's soul,—I would scarcely venture to
say so much, had not Bossuet led the way—
" If I tell you that Jesus rising from the sepul-
chre is a pledge of our resurrection, I shall
only tell you a truth which every Christian
knows ; but if I add that this great and divine
work is already begun in our mortal bodies,
you will perhaps wonder, and will find it hard
to understand, how in our corruptible bodies,
God is already carrying on the work of their
blessed immortality.

" Hearken, dust and ashes, and be glad in
the Lord ;—whilst this mortal body is crushed
with weakness and infirmity, God is already
sowing in it the seeds of an unchangeable existence, whilst it is growing old God is renew-
ing it, whilst it is daily exposed to dangerous
illness, and to certain death, the Holy Ghost
is providing for its glorious resurrection."

Is not this St. Paul's meaning in that wonderful text: " Glorify God, and carry God in
your bodies ?"

Here is the hope of the poor sufferer from
tedious illness; in the depths of his being, among
the very roots of his soul and body, God, by
His Holy Ghost, is sowing the seeds of the
resurrection of his body, and is beginning the
work of his blessed and unchangeable immortality. All this is being wrought in him by
the power and the blood of Him who is the
second Adam, the cause of our life, as the
first Adam is the cause of our death. Whilst
sickness and death, the work of the first Adam,
is going on within us, the second and life-
giving Adam is beginning His work. The

second Eve, Mother of life, is working within us; already the seeds of an unchangeable existence are germinating in our bodies. Here is enough, and infinitely more than enough to heal us even in this life, if we will be healed, if we can believe, and if the health of our body would be for the good of our soul. Otherwise the work of the first Adam will go on to its end. Still, beneath this dying flesh there are the seeds of immortality; there is a new man in our bosom, like a babe in the womb of its mother, and at the moment of our seeming death, this new man will shake off his shackles to live for ever.

Who can tell whether some day the increase of divine faith and the universal diffusion of a greater love of God, and of the pure Mother, by whom He deigned to come into the world, the Mother of life, and the health of the weak, will not draw down from God, for future generations, a fuller life, a more robust health of soul and body; and whether men will not find the principal support of life in a lively faith, in prayer and the sacraments, and in the holy unction which was established for the body as well as for the soul?

Who can tell whether these holy powers, when received and digested by the virtue which Mary gives—by humility, which replaces its life in its true centre, by chastity, which curbs, elevates, and transfigures its powers—by chastity which renews it as its source, and sends forth its cleansing and life-giving heat—who knows whether all these virginal powers will not bring to pass that

epoch of the world, which was foretold by a
great saint: " When there shall be but one
science of soul and of body, because the two
shall live the same life ?"

O Mary, health of the weak, pray for thy
servants. Grant us, O Jesus, the virginal
virtues; by means of them heal our infirmities,
whether of soul or body ; deliver us from the
sombre sadness of the present world, and
grant us the first fruits of eternal joy.

O Lord, I will from henceforth try to rule
my body with more prudence than I have
done hitherto. I know what a fool I have
been, I have indulged my sensuality instead
of curbing it ; I have not imposed on my body
the law of sacrifice, and that which Thou hast
said of the life of the soul, has proved true of
the life of my body. " He who will keep his
life, shall lose it, and he who consents to lose
it, shall find it." Fasting and prayer would
often have killed the seeds of disease, which I
fostered by dieting them: the more I nursed
my body, the more weak, feeble, and rebel-
lious it became. The more I would preserve
my life the farther it runs away ; the selfishness of the body is its ruin. The body, given
up to the inclination of its flesh, overloads
itself with foreign matter, surcharges itself, as
the Scripture says, and accumulates in itself a
clogged life, which the sacred text calls " a
thick mud." If I had denied my body, if I
had let it suffer for a time, I should have preserved its strength. I will be wiser for the
future. With all my heart I will renounce

my life, and even place it in thy hands, O
Health of the weak, that thou mayst offer it
to God, who is its well-spring, who alone can
renew it, can regenerate it, can fit it for eternity. I will no more devote to myself the
life of my body, and so make it more and
more earthly and corruptible ; but I will more
and more devote it to God, to make it incor-
ruptible and heavenly.

———

MEDITATION XXVI.

Seat of wisdom, pray for us !

If thou thus blessest our body, O beloved
protectress of mankind, how shall it be with
our soul, when thou deignest by thy virtues
to maintain it, and practise it in the works of
light ?

Humility, chastity, charity ! What a fund
for the future light and knowledge of man !
O Seat of wisdom, pray for us, that we may
escape from our darkness, our quarrels, our
parties, our childish inconstancy, and our
barbarous ignorance, and may attain to light
and peace, the peace of the wisdom and the
knowledge of God.

" We must know," says a pious and profound
writer, " that there are three kinds of science ;
the first is merely human, the second, purely
divine, and the third both divine and human.
The science of the pagans was merely human,

for they started from human principles, and depended only on their own efforts. Their study had no other than a natural end; such as the satisfaction of their own mind, the desire of their own perfection, or the honour and praise of men. There are but too many Christians who study in the same way.

"The purely divine and infused science, is one of the gifts of the Holy Ghost, and has been granted to the apostles and a multitude of other saints.

"The third is both human and divine, and is the real and true science of Christians, and that of which the wise man speaks when he says; 'God gave him the science of the saints, and completed his labours.' This is infused, but not without labour; it is both infused and acquired."

The science which we pray thee to obtain for us, O Mary, Seat of wisdom, who hast given the eternal Light to the world, is this true science of Christians: a science that is conformed to thy Son, who is both God and man, a science that proceeds both from God and from man,—from God, who inspires it by His light and His grace, and from man, who works and prays, who searches and profoundly meditates with the help of God's light and inspiration.

All the great doctors of the Church, and the theologians of the first rank, have had this kind of science, which has been sometimes also granted to women in the seclusion of their convents.

Never, perhaps, has anything more admira-

ble been written on the divine aspect of the
true science, and on the practical methods of
obtaining it, than the following noble exhorta-
tion of a holy woman who was favoured with
the inspiration of God.

"You, my people, whose religion is without guile, who have fixed your hearts on the
aim of overcoming the world, and of bearing
heaven within you, turn not back, persevere
in the way of vision which you have chosen,
and purify your eyes that you may be able to
raise them to the contemplation of the light,
where your Life and your Redeemer dwelleth.
This is the way to purify the eye of the heart,
and to give it power to raise itself to the true
light—to despise the cares of the world, to
mortify the body, to have a contrite heart, to
make pure and frequent confession of every
sin, and to wash it away with tears. And
after cleansing away all impurity, this is the
way to lift up the eyes, to meditate on the
unspeakable essence of God, and His awful
purity and truth; to pray forcibly and simply,
to rejoice in God, and to desire His kingdom.
Adopt this for your constant work. and press
on towards the light which God offers you as
His children, and which comes down sponta-
neously into your hearts. Take your hearts
in your hands, and offer them to Him who
speaks to you, and He will fill them with a
glory that shall make them partakers of the
divine nature, and you shall be children of the
light, and angels of God.

"Children of Adam, does it seem to you a
small thing to become children of God? Why

then turn away your faces from Him who giveth such power to men; you, especially, who have determined to dwell peaceably in this world, and to live like angels on the earth? You who are burning lights, whom the Master has placed on a hill to enlighten mankind, by your words and your examples, take heed lest pride and covetousness quench the light. Children of peace, stop your ears to the noise of the world, and make a deep silence within you, that you may listen to the Spirit who speaks to your heart."

Besides these religious efforts to obtain the divine part of science, you must employ the severe and persevering labour of a life. The patient comparative study of the mysteries of visible nature, the lessons of history, the grand tradition of the human mind, and especially the divine tradition of the Church, will ripen towards the autumn of your life into a science which is certainly better than the world can give.

Perhaps, O Mother of light, O Seat of wisdom, if Christians give themselves to thee by practising thy virtues more abundantly, then mankind towards the autumn of its history will attain to a knowledge more high, more wide, •more deep, than it has yet been able to reach.

Many saints have possessed the purely divine science; many pagans have possessed something of human science; Christians, not without the visible influence of the light and grace of Christ, have wonderfully developed human science: but the science which is at

once divine and human, which extends to the
universality of truths, has not yet been developed.   We find its germ in the theology
of the greatest doctors, but this germ, though
full of hidden life, has never yet been sufficiently nourished with material food, with the
elements of the visible world.   The time is
coming when this inferior subject matter of
science will be better prepared, and will be
open to the insight of the mind, and perhaps
will be subdued and penetrated by the supe-
rior element of science.

But where shall we find a mind capable of
taking in this whole, at once divine and
human ?   Where shall we find a body chaste
enough to endure the work, a mind large
enough to embrace the whole, and humble
enough to investigate every petty detail, and a
heart warm enough to give it the consecration
of love ?   O Mary, thy servants only for whom
thou hast obtained thy virtues of humility,
chastity, and charity, will be able to receive
this science at once divine and human, the
science of the age to come, of the kingdom of
God upon earth.   Some day, perhaps, education will not be so confined to the human side
of science, to those dry and technical lessons,
which are as it were, external fomentations
applied to the brain and memory of the child.

Perhaps the child Jesus, who requires of us
a different education for His Childhood, will
teach us, through thee, to discover the holy
germ which is laid up in the child's soul;
perchance, when the child questions us about
the voices he hears in his heart, about those

mysterious and deep whisperings which arouse
him and call him, about those distant glimpses
of light which he fancies he sees in the heaven
of his soul—perchance, we shall learn to do
more than answer him, like the High Priest
Heli : " It is nothing, go to sleep again."—
Perchance, we shall feel that we had better
open our eyes, as the high priest did at last
with the child Samuel, and like him, tell the
child, who does not yet know the secret voice
of God, " Go, and if you are called again, say
to God ; Speak Lord, for Thy servant heareth."

O Mary, Queen and Mother of children,
suffer not the world, with its shallow wisdom,
its dulness and its jeers, to quench in the
souls of children the germ of true science, the
source of divine wisdom, the light of inspiration. Rather let the voice of their teachers
inspired with thy maternal spirit, O Mother
of Christians, make these souls yet unfolded,
these understandings yet in the bud, realise
the words which the Holy Ghost speaks to
them ; " Listen to me, ye seed of God, grow
up like the rose tree planted by the water's
side, give forth your flowers and your perfumes like the lily, put forth your branches
of grace, and learn to praise God, and to bless
Him in all His works."

Perchance, O Mary, thou wilt obtain for us
the knowledge how to prepare the child's
mind to receive in due time knowledge and
wisdom.

I have been as blind to the interests of my
mind as to those of my body, O my God.

So far from seeking my mind's life, first in Thee, then in my soul, then in nature, I have inverted the whole order. I have recognised no means of learning but books, as I have recognised no means of strengthening my body but material food, without sufficiently considering the influences of the air, and of the spirit of nature; and still less, the influences of the soul, and the mighty power of God, that comes to me by prayer. In the same way, I have known no food for my mind, but that which my hands can touch and my eyes take in, books, and nature. I have not learnt to question my soul, still less to question God: if I had an insight into my soul, and into God, without neglecting the books through which other men speak to me, then I should understand the meaning of the books, and should read them in the spirit that dictated them, rather than in the letters which compose the words and syllables which I laboriously spell over, and find but a meagre outline of the living thought they represent.

But, O God, why have I no insight into my soul, and into Thee?

Because the soul must be pure, humble, chaste, and recollected, in order to be the mirror of God. For it is written: "Blessed are the pure in heart, for they shall see God."

If I had thy virtues then, O Mary, I should behold the light face to face: I should renew the life of my mind at its highest source.

Therefore, O Mother immaculate, I will give thee my mind as well as my body, that thou mayst offer me wholly, mind and body, to God.

———

MEDITATION XXVII.

Mother most amiable, and mother of pure love love, pray for us!

Mother most amiable, and Mother of pure love, pray for us, obtain for us a heart to love thee, to praise thee and to thank thee worthily for all the benefits which God bestows on the world through thee, and for those which He is reserving for the latter days of mankind upon earth.

By the spread of thy worship, and of the imitation, knowledge, and love of thee, we may yet hope for great improvements in the world, and for unspeakable benefits. But there is one improvement, one benefit that is greater than all, because it includes all, and this, O Mother of love, is the progress and spread of the love which thou givest. What would be the use of a progress of knowledge among men, without a still greater progress of love?

"Love," says St. Francis of Sales, "is a word that is misused and degraded, but it must be kept, for it is a word of incomparable beauty."

If all the law and the prophets are reduced to a single commandment; "To love God above all things, and thy neighbour as thyself,

for the love of God:" if St. Paul keeps ever
saying to us: " Love is the fulfilling of the
law ; the law is fulfilled in one saying, Love thy
neighbour:" if St. Augustine says, " Love
and then do what you like," we can see why
St. John, the Apostle of love, the first-born of
the adopted children of Mary, in his old age,
did but repeat one thing ; " My children, love
one another, for this is the commandment of
the Lord, and this by itself is enough."

But, O Mary, spotless and ever immaculate Virgin, who art therefore all lovely and
Mother of pure love, look whether in the midst
of our wickedness and deformity we are
worthy of being beloved, or able to love. Thou,
because thou art immaculate, art all beautiful ;
if the spot of sin, if only the fuel of sin had
been in thee but a single instant, even in thy
mother's womb, thou wouldst have retained
some trace of its deformity : thy soul would
have had its combats, not only against outward
evil, but against that which is within, and
these combats would have written their wrinkles
on thy brow.   But the Scripture says, thou art
all beautiful, without spot or wrinkle ; but we,
behold we are all ingrained with spots and
deformities ; O if we did but know what a
deformity is sin, how destructive of love is
wickedness !

Because thou art all fair before God, and
because thou art truly the Mother of pure love,
I know by an infallible reasoning, that thou
wast ever immaculate, and hadst no part even
in Adam's sin.   And because the dogma of
the Immaculate Conception is springing up

from its old roots, is growing high, spreading
its branches, and putting forth its matchless
blossoms and its wonderful fruits, we may
believe that the earth and mankind will become more beautiful, and men more capable,
and more worthy of love.

O amiable and admirable Mother, behold, I
beseech thee, our deformities, and take pity at
the sorry sight.

Behold our childhood sensualised, our youth
corrupted, our manhood effete, our old age
dried up before its time; behold the face of
mankind, purple or else ashy pale with its
passions, disfigured with the seven shapes of
sin, and their companion trains of sickness and
suffering; behold these eyes dulled or dissi-
pated, or ashamed, if not made still more
frightful by pride, lust, hatred or malice; ah
how seldom do we find among men those
placid eyes, soft yet strong, that are the tokens
of innocence, never lost, or if lost regained!
and when is it given to us to see those gracious inspired eyes of a soul which has an insight into God, and which beholds the world,
nature, and men, in God,—eyes which are
replete with all the rays of life, of courage, of
strength, of goodness, and of truth, because
they are like the soul, and the soul is like
God? Does not the Sun of justice pour forth
His rays and His beauties upon all souls? He
sheds them, but we quench them all; we will
not let our faces reflect the face of God, as
He would have them. O Mother immaculate,
the only perfect beauty, who hast never
quenched a single ray of God's light, who hast

shed and still sheddest the eternal light upon
the world, pray for us. And though we are
not lovely because we are hideous, yet at least,
O Mother of pure love, make us loving. Thy
Son has given us commandment to love, not
to be loved. And, O Jesus and Mary, ye by
loving us, by loving the lowest of mankind,
the poorest, the weakest, the most leprous, and
the most deformed, have shown us how to love
those who are not lovely. Moreover, ye show
us the way to do it, and this is, to love
them in God.

What is the meaning of loving things in
God, but to look at them in God, to invest
them with the beauty which they have in God,
and which God seeks to give them, and will
give them in His glory? Is it not certain
that those who carry in their hearts some rays
of God's light, and whose refined senses penetrate more easily through the body to the soul,
through the soul to God—is it not true that
hearts of this kind see through the human
countenance and eye the character of the soul,
and the ideal of beauty which it may realise
in God? Do they not feel an unutterable love
for that which has such possibilities of beauty,
and do they not leap for joy when they see a
soul making a free and clear-sighted effort
towards the realization of the model which
God proposes to it?

O amiable and admirable Mother, Mother of
holy love, may we presume to say more?

I see everywhere in the world, and throughout history, that the progress of Christianity
and of thy worship was ever followed by the

progress of love, in every sense of the word.
And surely, this progress begins low enough,
for we see races which eat men's flesh, and
which, in the drunkenness of their brutal passions, lose all traces of love. How many
men still live in this savage state!

The civilized pagans are not cannibals,
but they slay for their pleasure. Their fes-
tival enjoyment is in the bloody shows of
gladiators, and it is impossible to say how
degraded and perverted their senses have
become.

As for the Christian ages, they vary according to their purity and their faithfulness
to God; but in comparison to infidels and
savages, Christians are mildness and charity
itself.

This is the origin of that hearty and intelligent love, of which St. Francis of Sales speaks.
It exhibits traces of the eternal love which
shall unite souls in God; as for example, the
love of the same St. Francis, the apostle of
kindness, towards that soul whose "vigor-
ous heart" he somewhere praises. His love
inspired her with the supernatural power of
giving birth to a new order in the Church.
When he died, his love left her not, his eyes
still watched his beloved sister; as she was
dying he came to meet her, he was the angel
whom God sent to receive her soul, and carry
it to heaven. O Mother of pure love, this is
the kind of progress which the heart of man
asks of thee, that heart ill at ease, and moan-
ing either for the privation or deprivation of
love. Man's heart, so full of stains, is the

9

old vessel of which Scripture speaks, wherein
the wine of the new love cannot be kept
without the wine fermenting and corrupting,
the vessel bursting, and the wine being spilt.
If none is put in, does it fare any better with
the old vessel? It dries up, and shrivels, and
cracks.   Man's heart, then, must first learn
to purify itself by giving itself to thee, O
immaculate Virgin, that it may be again
worthy and capable of love.

Thou art that matchless and ever new
vessel wherein the wine remains without a
shadow of corruption, because thou art immaculate from the first instant of thy being.
Never was there the least mixture of the old
leaven in thee; for this thou wast made
spouse of the Holy Ghost, and the Mother of
eternal love.   Therefore, O Mother of immaculate love, who hast more love than all
other creatures together, refresh us with some
drops of that new wine, that new love, which
men shall drink in the kingdom of heaven;
teach thy adopted children, as thou didst teach
St. John, teach us to love.   Educate thy whole
family, the Church, and extend it, if possible,
to all mankind, educate it like St. John, that
from age to age, and from year to year, it
may be united and transfigured in love.   Increase in the Church the devotion of the
Sacred Heart; teach us to unite our hearts to
that Heart, through thine; and as the food
which enters the blood of a man, enters it
through the heart, which gives not life, but
receives it, so teach us to enter into the Heart
of Jesus, and to be incorporated with His Blood

and His life, through thee, O Gate of heaven, who art the human side of the Heart of Jesus Christ.

O my God, why have I loved so much without Thee, instead of loving in Thee? Like my body and my mind, my heart has made a mistake. It has loved for itself, instead of loving for Thee. It seeks love without, instead of within, and in Thee.

Instead of loving Thee, I have loved Thy creatures; instead of loving Thy creatures in Thee, I have loved them in themselves, and in the basest parts of their being. I have loved them for their vanity, and not for their worth, I have loved them for that which vanishes, not for that which endures; I have not the real love of mind and heart.

O if I had the holy love which God gives through thee, O immaculate Mother, my heart would be no more empty or divided: it would not be empty, because I should love; it would not be divided, because I should have but one love. I should love Thee first, O my God, and then I should love in Thee all that I loved with the love of the understanding and of the heart.

All my love would then belong to my faith, to my religion and to my hopes of eternal life.

MEDITATION XXVIII.

Mary, our abode, pray for us!

Jesus and Mary, it is not easy to forego the meditation of thy heart when we have once tasted its sweetness; I say thy heart, Jesus and Mary, for ye have but one. As man's body has but one heart in two halves, so the kingdom of God has but one heart, the Catholic Church has but one.

The medals which represent the hearts of Jesus and Mary, one crowned with thorns, leaning on the other pierced with swords, fall short of the truth. Your two hearts are not merely in contact, they not only support each other—they are but one, like the two sides of the heart of man. To understand how really they are one, we must call to mind those striking revelations that have been made to various saints, who have seen Jesus take their hearts and dip them into His own, so that only one heart was seen, though the two remained distinct—we must call to mind how St. Vincent of Paul declared that he saw the soul of St. Francis de Sales in the shape of a ball of fire, coming from heaven to meet the soul of St. Jane Chantal; and how her soul, which was rising in the shape of another, but smaller fiery ball, mingled with the first, so that only one flame and one ball remained visible.

Doubtless this beautiful sphere, this double

star, ascended still higher, till it was united with the sovereign sun, the great centre of love, which is the heart of Christ, and that of His Mother, where the two sainted friends found their glory and their rest. Is not this the final consummation and the chief good which every heart hopes for? Alas! now we are separated, we are lonely, we are scattered; the hearts and souls which God created to form a living city, to live one life, since the fall are scattered like the leaves in autumn that have fallen from the boughs, and are divided from the tree.—Dead leaves, they may lie in heaps at the tree's foot, or fly in crowds with the windy gusts; but, however they may fly together, the sapless things can never again be one, and however thickly they may lie, they are nothing but a heap of dung.

"Who," cried St. Augustine, " who will lay hold on me? who will gather me from the midst of this dispersion? Who will re-unite me to the breast of our common mother, the holy city of heaven? O mother, who will gather me to thee?" And the Church cries out to the holy Virgin in the name of all God's children, "Holy Mother of God, we all dwell in thee, and we all leap for joy."* That is to say, our hearts and souls ought to have their dwelling in the heart and soul of the Mother of God, penetrated and enveloped as it is by the Word, and all His radiance, as the body of the sun is penetrated with light and heat, and enveloped with its rays.

* Sicut lætantium omnium nostrum habitatio est in te, Sancta Dei Genetrix.

Yes, O Lord, those who love know well what it is for soul to dwell within soul. Through Thee, who art simplicity itself, and in whom there is no division, all things may touch, and one soul may dwell in another: even here, mothers know, or might know, if they were as clear-sighted as they are loving-hearted, that after bearing their child in their womb, they bear its soul in their own during its infancy and childhood, by a union which sometimes is never dissolved, or the dissolution of which for many a mother is the loss of all joy, a desolation for which there is no cure but death. As for the Mother of God, our Mother, her heart is large enough for all men; its veins and its arteries extend to all the living. O that this union might never be broken for any of us; O that it might rather extend to those that are asleep, that it may draw us all closer, and that we may all at last find a home in this heart of the world, united to the heart of God in heaven !

We are told that the visible heavens offer us a sort of figure and foreshadowing of these things in the grand order and laws of creation. At the present time worlds and suns are dispersed in space like atoms of dust; but, say some of our learned men, this dispersion will not go on for ever. There is a common centre which attracts all things, and to which all created matter will one day be united. The earth and the planets, which travel through space, and which for thousands and thousands of years have been revolving round their brilliant sun, as a vessel might revolve round an island of light and fire,—all these bodies, they say, will at some time be again joined to the sun, and the sun himself, gravitating towards a still larger centre, will there be absorbed. The forces which maintain the heavenly bodies in their course being shaken, as the Gospel expresses it, in God's own time, the stars shall fall from heaven, and shall go to build up the one paradise, in the centre of the universe, at the foot of the throne of God, at the feet of her who compasses the eternal sun, and who is crowned with stars.

Whatever may be said of this idea, nevertheless it is certain that at the end of all things, as St. Thomas, following St. Peter and the Prophet Isaias, says, The world shall be renewed, and the creation transformed by fire; we shall be together in that place, of which our Lord says: "I go to prepare a place for you;" we shall be in that great city, of which He says in another place: " I will that where I am all they that love me may be likewise."

Then shall be formed the new heavens and the new earth, which was announced by the Prince of the Apostles, and foretold by the prophets; an eternal world, where justice shall dwell, where there shall be no more tears, nor evil, nor death, because God will wipe away tears from every eye, because all hearts shall be united amongst each other, and with God, and thus everything shall be bound up in eternal love, and eternal and immutable perfection.

O when shall we come to this world of

unity, where there shall be no more evil, nor
fear of death, where God will wipe away the
tears from all eyes, where we all shall be
united together in God?

Here we are all in disunion. The members
of the human race are placed at such distances
in time and space that the greater part will
never see one another. Among those who
live with me here below, how few have I ever
looked at even once! And those whom I do
see, pass by, and I see them no more. I meet
them on the road, I salute them, and this
salutation is but an eternal farewell. In this
way do the sons of Adam, who live at the
same time, pass by each other in this life,
without speaking, without knowing one
another. And those who do know one
another, who converse together, and believe
that they live together, are often still further
separated in mind and heart, than men who
never see nor speak to each other. O this
cannot be our country! This is not the man-
sion of the Father of the family. This is not
the abode where those who love shall be united
amongst themselves and with God. This is
not the bosom of our heavenly Mother, where
we are all to be gathered together. Let us
pass on till we reach the place of repose. But
let us walk towards our true end; let not the
heart deceive itself and take a wrong road.
One love alone leads us travellers to our country, to the abode of eternal love: it is that
which loves all in God, and which gives itself
to the immaculate Mother, that it may be

continually exalted and consecrated, till it is swallowed up in God.

———

MEDITATION XXIX.

Mary our hope, pray for us.

O how slow are we to comprehend the meaning of these words of the Salve Regina: " Our life, our sweetness and our hope, all hail !" Who understands the full sense of these words : " Mary our hope !" May we now, by the grace of God, meditate on them sufficiently to get a glimpse of their truth.

What is hope ? What is the meaning of this charming word ? What constitutes this powerful virtue ?

Men think they know it, for they live on hope. No one dwells in the present, every one turns to the future, where he expects to see better days.

We live not, we do but hope to live: as St. Paul says : " Every creature groans, as it waits." But how often are we deceived by vain hopes, which lead us astray here below ! Sometimes I hope for what I shall never obtain ; sometimes I hope for that which will bring me no happiness. Do I then hope too much ? Must I live without hope ? O that men knew that their hopes are vain, precisely because they hope too little ! They hope without energy, and they hope for too small a happiness. Hope abundantly, absolutely. Hope for the perfect possession of all possible good, and you will not be deceived. Hope, which is full and unwavering, is infallible.

O if we had a firm belief in this! If we knew of a truth that hope which is absolute is infallible, that is to say, that the perfect assemblage of all possible good is a present reality, and that man, whatever he may be, can and ought to possess this full and sovereign beatitude!

Yes, my God, Creator of the world, and sanctifier of intelligent and free creatures, Thou hast willed that thus it should be. Thou hast willed that besides Thyself, who art infinite happiness and absolute perfection, there should exist creatures capable of sharing Thy happiness and Thy perfection. Thou hast created them, and Thou hast called them to this divine participation; and as for this it was necessary to create them free beings, for they alone would be capable of sharing Thy happiness and perfection, and as free beings could sin, and stain themselves with impurities, and make themselves every way unworthy of the hope set before them, Thou hast provided from the stores of Thy infinite power a redemption to restore life to beings worse than dead, to raise up creatures that had fallen miserably. For this Thou hast wrought, O God, a wonderful work; through Thy incarnation, or to prepare for it, Thou hast provided that in the midst of the spirits Thou didst create, all of whom might fall into

sin, there should be a pair pure enough to
regenerate all mankind, the soul of the God-
M n, and the soul of the immaculate Mother
of God—One, of which we can only say that
it is one with God ; the other, of which we may
say that without losing its liberty it possesses
the highest conceivable degree of purity after
that of God. So that, beneath Thee, Ô God,
who art the infinite and uncreated perfection,
and beneath Thee, O Christ, perfect God and
man, there is at the head, or in the centre of
mankind, a being whom we may call the rela-
tive and created perfection. Hence it follows
that in the order of perfection all that is conceivable exists ; there is no gap. And not only
does all perfection and happiness which man
can imagine exist actually—infinite happiness
and uncreated perfection ; all imaginable created perfection, and all happiness of which a
creature is capable,—but the man who imma-
gines these things must at the same time believe that all this may be his, and that its
possession is offered to him. So that he can
never imagine any thing too beautiful or too
happy ; and the only fault his hope can have
is to be too timid.

Still we do not yet see the whole mystery,
beauty and greatness of Christian hope. Let
us go a step further. If faith, as St. Paul
says, is the substance of things hoped for,
what will hope be ? For hope, though less
than charity, is greater than faith. Is not
hope also the substance of good things to come ?
What is the real principle of faith, hope, and
charity, the divine virtues which God only

infuses into the soul ?   Their principle is grace.
And what is grace, but the beginning of our
participation of the divine nature ; our first
entrance on the possession of God?   And
what is this first entrance on the possession of
God, but the beginning of eternal life, and of
sovereign happiness ?   So that Christian hope
already holds what it hopes for, it holds it in
principle, in substance, in beginning, in germ,
as the doctors who follow the Scriptures teach
us.

"We are partakers of Christ," says St.
Paul, "if we hold fast within ourselves the
beginning of His substance, even to the end ;"
yes, Jesus Christ is in His sanctuary, and this
sanctuary is our soul, if we always hold fast
in ourselves this glorious hope, even to the
end.   It is of this beginning, and this substance
of the life of Jesus in man, that St. John says,
" the divine seed dwelleth in him."

But how hold fast this glorious hope, even
to the end, in the midst of all our toil, weakness, and sin?   O Mary, our hope, help us to
know it.   O holy Mother of God, immaculate
Queen, show us how thou art the Mother of
holy hope, how thou art the encouragement,
the protection and the foundation of hope.

There are two beautiful sayings of St.
Ambrose and St. Anselm, which will show us
the way.   "O that the soul of Mary," says
St. Ambrose, "might be in each of us to glorify
God, that the spirit of Mary might be in us,
to rejoice in God !"

"Yes, she bears us all in her heart," says
St. Anselm, "as a true Mother."

"We all dwell in thee, full of joy, O holy Mother of God," says the Catholic Church.

But we must believe these things; we must understand that though matter is impenetrable, soul is not so.

There may be a mutual inter-penetration of all human souls; thus the spirit of Mary may penetrate the souls of her children, and all of them may be in her, and are in her.

Through this wonderful union of our souls with thine, O Mother, thou mayst stimulate, uphold, and direct our hope. Thou mayst stimulate it by telling us, when God's grace calls us, how much better is that which He offers than that which we seek. Thou mayst rule it by ever correcting us when, after having chosen God's side, we seek Him where He is not. Thou mayst uphold it steadfastly in us even to the end, whenever our soul wearied with its repeated faults and failures is tempted to lose sight of perfection, and to renounce holiness. Then it is, O Mother, that thou whisperest to the soul of thy child; Be brave, be strong, thou mayst still overcome. Holiness is still held out to thee, perfection still offered. What is more, O beloved Mother, sometimes thou showest us in sweet inward vision a wonderful sight, which is at once our soul itself, and the idea which God has of it, and the degree of perfection to which He wishes to raise it; and thy fundamental virtues seem lent to it for a moment, and at the same time something of thy ravishing beauty is reflected in it, some feature of thine wherein each of us may come to resemble his heavenly Mother.

Yes, to give us courage and raise our desires to heaven, thou showest us our soul for a moment transfigured in thine own, and in God; thou showest us the beauty and glory of which we are capable, and which is in store for us if we persevere. Who has not sometimes fancied he saw his soul dwelling in light, in peace, in life, in that beauty which comes from wisdom? I know that hell can also show us false portraits of the soul, which are sufficiently flattering to intoxicate pride by their malicious and guilty beauty, and sufficiently hideous to excite the horror and disgust of any one who has caught a glimpse of the beauty of holiness. These illusions, these perverse pictures, cause a momentary feeling of unbounded pride, which is followed by a speedy and complete prostration. But when thou, O Mother, showest us our souls transfigured in the halo of light which God has given thee, thou dost but impress on our hearts, and engrave on our memories a loving remembrance of heaven, a clear and humble knowledge of our earthly deformity, and a magnanimous resolution to overcome all, that we may wash out our sins and regain our glory.

Thus it is, O Mother of souls, that thou dost rally our hope, thou who art our hope. If we could but understand this truth to the full!

" I am the Mother of pure love, and of holy hope," the Scripture makes thee say. " In me is all hope of life and of virtue; he that eateth me shall yet hunger, and he that drinketh me shall yet thirst." Compare this with what our Saviour says: "Blessed are they that hunger, and thirst after justice ; for they shall have their fill ;" and again : "He that eateth me shall hunger no more, and he that drinketh of the water that I shall give him, shall never thirst."

By placing these two passages together, we discover something of the mystery of the holy Communion. No creature can live, without some communion with God; but no soul can have eternal life, but by the real communion of the divinity, the soul and the body of Jesus Christ. Now there is as it were a preparatory communion which gives a heavenly hunger, and there is the communion itself which gives paradise ; and the soul grows with its appetite for that sacred food, which gives life more and more abundantly, as our Saviour says. And this growth of appetite is nothing but that opening of our heart which God ever requires from those who love Him,—" Open your heart, and I will fill it."

God, then, ever requires that our heart should open itself wider the more life it receives, in order that it may receive still more. God gives an increase of life whenever a new impulse of hunger craves for it ; and then, we reconcile the two texts, " He who feeds on me has still hunger :" and, "He who feeds on me shall never hunger." For this heavenly food is of two kinds ; one increases the hunger and thirst for life, the other satisfies all hunger and quenches all thirst. One opens the heart, the other fills it ; the first is the created

wisdom, who says: "He who feeds on me,
is still hungry; the other is the uncreated
Wisdom, which says: "He who feeds on me,
shall never hunger more."

Therefore, O holy Mother of God, it is thou
who givest us, or rather conveyest to us, this
heavenly hunger. When we imitate thy humility and thy purity, thou becomest the human
preparation for our substantial communion with
God. To partake of God is our life and our
highest good, and thou, by thy humility and
purity, art the hunger and thirst after God.
Therefore thou art the hope of happiness and
of life; and if Christian life, is all summed up
in the Holy Communion worthily received, if
the worthy reception depends entirely on our
preparation, and if thou art our preparation,
what place dost thou hold in the work of our
salvation? Now I understand the pious
opinion: "He who loves thee, O Mary, cannot perish." It is thou that enlargest our
souls, and openest our hearts, for the hunger
and thirst after God; by thy prayers and thy
example we can make those aspirations for
life, those expansions of heart, which invite
God to come to us, and increase His
presence within us, which are the hope and
the growth of life. Truly, then, O Mother,
thou art our hope.

When we are united to thy soul and thy
spirit, and the words of St. Ambrose are fulfilled,—"May the soul of Mary be in her servants to increase the presence of God in them;
may the spirit of Mary be in her servants, to
rejoice in God;"—our soul, united to this great

soul, to this spirit which soars so high, understands what true greatness is, feels its own
littleness and vileness, and is humbled. The
moment it enjoys this greatness, it sees and
feels all possible greatness, the infinite perfections of glory; and in this vision, that which
it already has seems nothing; it desires, and
hungers after a more abundant life, it is humble, it perceives its littleness, and prays that it
may increase; like St. Paul, it forgets what
is behind, and reaches forward to that which
is before, and hastens to meet its life. And
this is hope, that heavenly hope and greatness of
soul which exclaims: "My soul doth magnify
the Lord, and my spirit has leaped forth in
God," (exultavit). This is the song which
ascends and shall ascend eternally from the
heart of her who is our succour and our hope.

Happy is the soul that bears this song
within itself,—that hears in regions higher
than its height, and deeper than its depth, the
voice of hope calling it to more mysterious
depths of humility, and to more sublime
heights of development, beneath the eye of
God, which glorifies all that it looks upon.

O Mother of hope, in whom all hope is
found, stimulate, guide, and ever increase in
me this blessed virtue. Never permit me to
acquiesce in my misery, or to despair of becoming better; never permit me to be contented with the virtue I have, however great
it may be, or to be satisfied with its measure.
Ever show me how small it is, and ever give

God, art this Sun of glory. In praising me ever more and more, the holy Church glorifies Thee, O my Saviour; I transmit this glory to Thee, I keep nothing back, for what have I to do with Thee, with Thee who art All, while I in Thy presence am nothing ?"

O Jesus, Lamb of God, who takest away the sins of the world; in glorifying Thy holy Mother, whom have we glorified but Thee? For who made that immaculate purity, who took away the sin of Mary before she came into being? Who predestinated the second Mother of mankind, their true Mother, to the glory of crushing the serpent's head? Who gave her this power?

Thou only, O Jesus, Thou who takest away the sins of the world, and who workest this wonder to preserve it from future sin. Thou didst redeem beforehand the Queen of the world from sin, that Thou mightest show forth Thy master-work of a perfect creature, immaculate in her origin, immaculate in all her life, and for all eternity.

O Jesus, suffer us this day to meditate on this mystery in Thy presence, or rather tell us Thyself how Thou dost take away the sins of the world, how the chief and master-piece of Thy divine work is Thy immaculate Mother; speak to us concerning this mystery some of those words which are spirit and life.

Jesus. "In the beginning, My son, I, the eternal Word, with the Father and the Holy Ghost, spoke, saying: 'Let us make man in our image, after our likeness;' and as a word of thine, O My son, is heard by thou-

sands of thy fellow-men around thee, this
word of Our mouth was heard by all the beings
whom We ordained to life, by all the souls
whom I meant to hear it,—and all who heard
it live.

" For thee, O My son, and for every soul
of man, this word is the life which I give, and
which I am ever offering thee. This day,
this moment, I am speaking this word for
thee, and if thou livest, if thou thinkest, if
thou lovest, it is because thou still hearest
it. If I ceased speaking, thou wouldst cease
being; but in this simple word of My mouth,
thou mayst hear two distinct things; thou
hearest the word which makes thee man,
and thou art free to hear that which would
make thee a child of God: thou hearest that
which gives thee thy natural life, and thou
oughtest to hear that which takes away thy
sins, and gives thee the life of grace. That
which I speak, I speak everlastingly; I speak
not like thee, by intervals; My words do not
die away every moment, like thine; My
words are lasting, are fixed, are eternal, and
I no more cease pronouncing over thee the
word which creates and regenerates thee, which
gives thee or offers thee the twofold life of
nature and of holiness, than the sun ceases to
enlighten and to warm the worlds which
revolve around it.

" But, O My son, We never meant that Our
grand, creative, and sanctifying word should
remain a single instant without its full effect.
We made it abundantly true when we said:
' Let us make man to our image and likeness;'

truth, affection, and holiness; to whom I ought
ever to correspond with love and understanding; do I not pass my whole life without
answering Thee, or listening to Thee?   O my
Master and my God, when have I ever decidedly and fully corresponded to Thee?"

Jesus. " My son, this is thy sin! In the
narrow bounds of thy sickly soul, which knows
not how to come to Me, and to go out of
itself, thou hast contracted the evil habit of
listening little, and answering less. And these
answers, which might at any moment of thy
life sanctify thee, and gain heaven for thee ;—
I wait for them, sometimes for long years,
sometimes for a whole life; and all the while
thy soul is dwelling in the land of sleep and
death.   Yet this death of sin do I destroy, at
thy first true answer to My voice.   Mark My
words: I am ever saying to thee, O soul, I
create thee to Our image, after Our likeness;
but then I wait for thy answer.   To be dumb,
or to contradict, is thy sin.   But if after I
have borne forty years thy silence of sleep and
of death, thou givest Me but one answer, then
all thy sins are blotted out.

" If I give thee all these days, all these
hours, all these beats of thy heart, it is only
that thou mayst one day say to Me in
earnest, Yes my God, and that thou mayst
be regenerated by the answer which I call
forth.   I have governed the life of many
a man for a century and more, in order
that his soul may at last come to hear Me,
and give Me an answer.   Behold the long-

suffering and the patience of the Lamb of God, who taketh away the sins of the world."

The Soul. "Therefore, O Lord, lengthen the life of all men, until they give Thee this answer."

Jesus. "My son, the longer they live the more hardened do they become, in the habit of not listening. Thou knowest it well. The child answers me better than the old man; and this is why I gather like flowers their innocent souls into My garner. In time the heart becomes so hardened that I know it will never listen; then there is nothing left but to pronounce judgment.

"But thou canst not understand the greatness and the multitude of the means whereby I seek to awaken their souls, and to make them answer Me."

The Soul. "Teach me, O Lord, that I may understand it."

Jesus. "O My son, I am intimately present with the whole soul; I am in it always, and everywhere. I am present when it sins, and I hinder its sin from slaying it, and casting it down to hell, by upholding it even in the midst of its wickedness, which I wash away so far as My infinite power can wash it.

"But thou canst not yet comprehend Me. Sin is an infinite evil, for it separates the soul from its God, from the principle of its life; and this for ever. Through sin a great gulf yawns between the soul and its God, which it can no more pass over than it can create itself. By sin the soul merits eternal death, and is dead for all eternity.

10

" But that which the soul cannot do, its
Creator can ; I can pass over the infinite gulf ;
I can pass over to the soul.

" Though I am always everywhere present,
yet when the soul can no longer hear Me, I
may be said not to be there. I no longer
exist for it, I am, as it were, divided from it
by the infinity of My Godhead. But I can
pass over the gulf ; and by My incarnation I
present Myself to the soul, and I take its sins
upon Me.

" Then it comes to pass that the soul can
hear Me ; when I say to it, with a voice both
human and divine ; ' Thou art my image and
likeness,' it can hear Me, and its sins are
blotted out. And here the Church teaches
thee the history of My work, and the numberless contrivances of My wisdom, to take away
the sins of the world.

" This plan was conceived from all eternity,
and though simple in My eyes, to thine it has
two sides. Thou seest My aim, which is to
wash away thy sins, and to raise thee up to
everlasting life. But in My eternal wisdom,
the existence of the God-Man was by itself the
end and aim, as some of My saints have seen
and taught. When the Father, the Word, and
the Spirit say ; ' Let us make man after our
image and likeness,' their eternal will is to give
to these words their full, eternal, and infinite
meaning. In their full, perfect, eternal, and
infinite meaning their truth is fulfilled in Me
only, the God-Man, and Saviour of the world.
At the same time, My all-perfect and immaculate soul, which is united to Me, so as to be

but one Person with Me, was the means whereby I chose to come again into the world to unite Myself with human nature, to descend into it and to save it. Nevertheless, the Father, the Son, and the Holy Ghost, willed that the Son of God, God and Man, should be born of a Mother like men. And as it was Our will that the words which created mankind, should be perfectly and infinitely fulfilled in the God-Man, We willed also that they should be fulfilled completely though not infinitely in the creature. And thus it was part of the eternal plan of My work that another soul besides Mine—the soul of the Mother of God—should be a perfect and spotless image, and a faultless likeness of the Father, the Son and Holy Ghost. And this soul was the second aim of My work. The first was the God-Man, the perfect and infinite fulfilment of the creative Word; the second is the Mother of God, the perfect, but finite fulfilment of the same Word. All My wisdom is poured out on this twofold master-piece—a work altogether worthy of Me, than which no greater is conceivable, for on the one hand, it is God, and on the other, it is created perfection, the highest conceivable after God.

" Now learn, My son, what is an immaculate soul. It is a soul which, in that part of its life which depends upon itself, as well as upon Me, has always given a full response to every vibration of My voice. And these vibrations, quicker than those of light, must ever have found the soul attentive and ready to respond, —never has there been a refusal or a delay.

While in that part of the soul's life, which
depends not upon itself, in that depth where
neither reason nor free-will penetrates; never
has the effect or the impulse of sin or satan,
directly or indirectly, printed spot, or wrinkle,
or fault, or evil motion. Never has the least
movement, whose origin is evil, been experienced or allowed a passage through this
soul, even involuntarily. And this was needful,
O My son, for the slightest movement of evil
has its eternal consequences, and contributes to
form the fire of hell, and adds strength and
speed to the horrible eddies of the fiery lake.
In the soul which answers Me, I blot out these
motions and these sins, but it remains an eternal truth, that the soul has sinned, whether
actually or originally; that it is not immaculate, and has not the highest perfection after
God. There are but two souls that have this
perfection, two souls that were ever immaculate, that of the God-Man, and that of the
Mother of God. The third aim of My work,
and of Our creative word, was the assembly
of saints and of just men, whom I have saved
from death, by making them hear Me through
My incarnation or My inspirations, and to
whom My words apply: 'The time cometh
when they that are in their graves, shall hear
the voice of the Son of Man, and those who
hear it shall live.'

" In the sin of these souls, there was a bot-
tomless abyss and an infinite evil. My sacrifice and the infinite worth of My Blood, fills up
the abyss. I apply the price which takes
away sin to these men, fallen and dead to eter-

nal life, as Eliseus applied his living body to
the child to raise it to life.   The prophet laid
his hands over the child's little hands, his
body over the child's body, and his mouth on
its mouth, and breathed his breath into it.   I
do all this, and more; I mix My flesh and
blood with their flesh and blood ; My blood
circulates in their veins, and inwardly and
outwardly I apply My whole body to theirs.
My human spirit is mixed with theirs, My
soul with theirs, and whilst My soul speaks to
their soul, and My Spirit to their spirit ; and
whilst my blood flows in their veins, I make
them one with Me, and attract them to Me,
and for them and with them, I never cease to
raise towards Myself and towards My Father,
My soul, My spirit, and My body, with their
body, soul, and spirit attached to Mine.   As I
became Man by taking a soul and body, and
in raising up human nature to Myself, so I
become each one of them, by taking their body
and their soul for My dwelling-place, that I
may raise them up to heaven.   And these ap-
plications of My human nature, and through it
of My divine nature, to each person, are diver-
sified by the varied riches of My grace, and by
the visible forms of the sacraments.

"And as all My mysteries are eternal, I
made My inspired disciple call Me, 'The Lamb
slain from the foundation of the world.'
From the beginning, before Adam fell, My
blood washed and preserved her who was to be
My Mother, and the Mother of redeemed
mankind.

"The source of sin mounts not up to My

throne, its rise is far below the throne of My Immaculate Mother;—a privilege ineffable in its sublimity, in its wisdom, in its far-spread beneficence, in its application to her whose consent to her divine maternity, and whose merits I foresaw, those merits which, by My grace, made her worthy to bear her God.

"This, O My son, is the meaning of Our creative word pronounced at the beginning of time: 'Let us make man to our own image and likeness.' Thou seest that this word is fulfilled in an infinite degree in Me, the God-Man, thy Saviour and thy God; in a perfect and admirable degree in My Immaculate Mother, and in a true and admirable degree, though less full, in all the just and in My saints. And thou seest, as a mystery indeed, though not without some clearness, how Our divine word prevents or remedies the falling away of man from the likeness of God, and how it preserves from every stain of sin the pair that regenerates the world. Thou seest how, by My labours and sufferings, which I took upon Me to make My word heard by those who sleep, it blots out the sins of the world."

The Soul. "My Lord and my God, I hear Thee, I adore Thee, I love Thee! But this is the cry of my soul, listen to it! My God, have mercy on me! Lamb of God, wash me from my sins, wash away the sins of the world. Blot out my past sins, blot out my future sins. Preserve us from sin evermore, as Thou didst preserve Thy Mother from all sin. Take away the sins of the world, and prevent all future sin."

Lord, Thou hast spoken, and still speakest Thy mighty word, which creates us and regenerates us to Thy likeness. If I listened to this word, if the world would listen, any moment would suffice to regenerate my soul and the whole world in light and love. But death, which I cannot make up my mind to renounce, and to which the world clings, death does not hear Thy voice; and the waves of life pass over us and through us, without quickening us. Each new sin, each new degradation in death, renders my return to life more impossible. At least, O Lord, let me this day make a league with Thee against future sins, mine own and those of the world. O that the world sinned less, O Lord, that it were less dead, less emptied of Thy presence. O that the world would cling to the brightness of the doctrine of the immaculate purity of the Mother of all living, to the wonderful changes wrought by devotion to her who is the mother of God, the perfect form and idea of God, and the faultless realization of the Word which created and sanctifies man. And here let us not miss the lesson which it most imports the world to know; that Thou art the Lamb who prevents the sins of the world, and how the world's future may be better than its past, more victorious over the death of sin, over the infernal obstacle to light and love.

Yes, O Jesus, herein lies our progress; the progress of the world and of the individual soul. Grant, therefore, that the Virgin's virtues and the Virgin's view of things may spread more and more in the world, through the

practical worship and hearty and intelligent
imitation of the spotless Virgin Mother of God.
May God by the power of the Virgin's virtues,
which draw Thee towards us, O Jesus, our
life, and for which Thou providest when Thou
blottest out our sins,—may God's presence increase in the world, may it live there and
reign there.   May He be no longer insulted
and crucified either in the secret heart, or in
the public streets, may He be no more despised
and trampled on in His poor, in His children,
in the sick, and in the ignorant.

And I think I see, O Lord, that the imitation of Thy immaculate Mother, and the devotion to her created perfection, is growing, and
will grow in the Church and in the world.   It
is Thy will, and mankind is making ready for
it.   Thou willest that this divine light should
be shed more bountifully than ever on the last
age of the world, which will be, I hope, the
longest.   Thou willest that it should ever grow
in fruitfulness and beauty, to wash away and
to prevent sin.

Thou willest, O Jesus, that mankind should
crowd more thickly to this standard of light ;
Thou willest that they should learn its lessons
of understanding, boldness, and hope.   Thou
willest that they should learn how God has
long ago given Himself, and that it only remains for man to accept and to understand
what he has ; how man can live in Thee, and
give birth to Thee, can add Thy blood to his
own, Thy mind to his, and Thy sacred · heart
to his heart ; through what channels, and by
what springs, life, truth, freedom, and love

come to the soul, and grow within it, and in the world; how the spread of the Virgin's virtues, the only ones that can receive God, is the salvation and the progress of the world; how we can and must dispose and rule the earth in justice and in truth; how in the regions above the human soul there exists, not only the infinite perfection of God, which might seem too remote from us, but also the perfection of the creature; yes, in the actual creation perfection is possible; it exists, it lives, it comes to us, it touches us, and by some hidden and wonderful connection, we touch it. The imagination of man, therefore, can never soar too high, man cannot hope too much; if he wants perfection, spotless and faultless perfection, it is there. The perfection of created man is known by its name, and we know how to communicate with it. If we want more, if beyond this immaculate perfection we want a perfection that verges towards God's infinity, it is there, for we are told that the holy and immaculate perfection is Mother of God, and unites God to the world, and that God willed to become man in her womb to raise up mankind to Himself, and to kindle in him light upon light for ever and ever.

MEDITATION XXXI.

Lamb of God, who takest away the sins of the world, grant us Thy peace.

Lamb of God, who takest away the sins of the world, aid us in these anxious days, and blot out some, at least, of the most terrible consequences of our crimes. Quench our wrath, calm our hatred, stay our threats, and instead of the sounds of war, give us the fruitful stillness of labour. Lamb of God, grant us Thy peace.

Jesus, Lord of heaven and earth, when Thou dost ascend into heaven Thou sayest, "My peace I leave with you, my peace I give unto you;" and when Thou dost appear in the midst of us on the earth, Thou sayest, "Peace be with you."

O my God, Thou who art peace itself, is it not time, now nineteen hundred years after Thy coming, for peace, the glorious peace of justice, to begin its reign in the midst of the Christian world, and for the prayer of the Church to be fulfilled, which is ever asking for peace among Christian princes?

" When He is come," says Isaias, " the people shall beat their swords into ploughshares, and their spears into sickles: nation shall not lift up sword against nation, neither shall they be exercised any more to war." (Isaias ii. 4.)

When shall this be, O my God? when shall

we see the Gospel realized in the life of the nations?

When shall we see the life of nations multiplied by their union, and not neutralized by their wars?

When shall we see the nations remember that they are co-heirs of heaven, and members of one body?*

When shall we see the rulers become such as the Gospel speaks of, who, instead of oppressing their people with their extravagance and their wars, minister to them in justice and peace? (Matth. xx. 25.)

Or rather, when shall we see the people open their eyes, and rid themselves of the perpetual disturbers of the national life, the despisers of all government, the sacrilegious breakers of all laws, the overthrowers of dynasties and constitutions, and at the same time, by a natural consequence, learn to refuse to give to the head of the state, who can never be more than a man and an individual, the full power of the sword, of taxation, and of speaking, that is the power of regulating by himself all men's life, labour, and thoughts, and of determining by himself whether the world shall have war or peace?

When shall we see men understand the truth of the two great evangelical laws of history, "He that takes the sword shall perish by the sword," and "Blessed are the meek, for they shall possess the earth?" (Matth. v. 4, and xxvi. 52.)

* Gentes esse cohæredes et concorporales.—Ephes iii. 6.

When shall we understand that truth, justice, and goodness, have each, by itself, a kind of omnipotence, which wrath, war, and bloodshed can only lessen ?

· Thank God, the time draws near when men shall understand these things.

O Jesus, who takest away the sins of the world; who makest the Christian nations beyond comparison purer than the ancient world; who gavest them increase of science and reason, for the discovery of fresh means of subduing the earth ;—and who hast begun to give them some understanding of the excellence of peace: already hast Thou taught them to prize meekness and goodness; already in comparison with the barbarism and cruelty of old times, the Christian nations are as good, as meek, as peaceable as they are strong and enlightened.

Our eyes have seen for well nigh half a century a sight that was never before seen on earth—peace becoming a European institution, and war becoming year by year more difficult, and promising to become impossible. And when the last great war burst out we witnessed a compact of all nations to quench it as soon as possible. And even now, when peace has become unstable, we behold the nations, events and dieas, all conspiring with almost irresistible force to impose peace.

In these days when spaces are shortened, and Europe is as it were a single country; when there is daily intercourse of the nations with each other; when their labour and their wealth are inextricably intertwined; when

science, ideas, interests, manners, habits and
needs wreathe together all the nations into
one whole—this living and mighty whole will
not be torn and lacerated.   Knowledge, thank
God, everywhere conspires with the wisdom
and the love of men to banish war from the
bosom of our European father-land.

Nor is this all.   History and reason read
their comments on the gospel, and show us
the weakness of war and the strength of peace
to conquer and rule the world.

What do you want?   You want justice;
you want to deliver the oppressed.   History
and the Gospel show you that war always
increases the burden of the oppressed.   Now-
a-days no man who knows Europe can fail to
understand that among us, justice, truth,
knowledge, discussion, reason, opinion, and
moral and intellectual efforts, are stronger than
sword and fire.

All ye who suffer, and are oppressed, learn
to put your confidence, not in the sword which
ruins the cause that adopts it; nor in the
poniard, which stamps with infamy the cause
that tolerates it; but in the force of justice,
truth and faith, and in the quickening fire of
the heart of Jesus.

For oppression still exists among us, nation
oppresses nation, and citizens oppress each
other : O Jesus, Thou who didst come to deliver man, grant us that ardent love for the
oppressed which may be called Thy fire, the
fire which Thou didst kindle upon earth,* and

* Ignem veni mittere in terram, et quid volo nisi ut accenda-
ur ?—Luc. xii. 49.

show us at the same time, O Jesus, that this fire whose triumph is the one thing Thou didst desire,—is that mighty force which is to deliver us by changing all obstacles into sources of heat and light.

O my brother, didst thou never feel in thy youth that energy of conviction, that heaving of heart which seemed able to move the world? At that moment thou hadst a glimpse of the strength of justice and of faith; the sacred fire was kindled within thee. By this force, says the gospel, we can move mountains, and nothing is impossible to us. (Matt. xvii. 19.)

Why is this?

It is because God is everywhere. God the foundation of the world and the support of souls—God who is justice itself, dwells in the midst of each soul. Through this central medium mankind are in communion with each other, from one end of the world to the other. Through it the movements of thought are passed from man to man. All created spirits communicate with each other in God, who is justice and truth, ever present to the spirit and conscience of every man. When a man's will is fixed on justice and his thought on truth, this thought or will is a motion which is passed and propagated like light: it is a wave which gathers strength as it goes, which collects force from every consciousness, from every law of nature, and from God Himself who is the absolute force. When many men unite in one will, and in one belief, in the light of truth, and in the out-spoken honesty of evident and disinterested justice, and in the enthusiastic love of virtue; then the irresistible impulse of these intelligent and free multitudes, who form invisible armies, overturns every obstacle, and governs the world.

Of a truth, the wrath of man fulfils not the justice of God : but the peaceable, patient and persevering insurrection of the mind, the conscience and the heart in behalf of justice is an irresistible force, which is now more than ever all-sufficient. By this force, the just and the good shall become masters of the world, and shall overcome every power which resists the justice of God ; as where St. Peter, with a single word, struck the liars dead, or rather, as when Jesus, who is justice itself, made the soldiers fall to the ground, by simply saying to them : " I AM HE."

This is the force of the present age, to overcome the will by justice and the mind by reason, but not with sword and fire. This is the holy war of the ages to come ; this is the consecrated weapon of lawful revolutions.

O Jesus, Lamb of God, who takest away the sins of the world, grant us Thy peace, that we may live under Thy law, in Thy strength, in Thy truth, and in Thy freedom. Tell us again that if we keep Thy commandments, we shall know the truth, and the truth shall make us free. Show us that Thy sacred fire is kindled on the earth, and that its bright and mighty flame is all-sufficient to triumph peaceably over all things.

But it must be kindled and must shine forth,

or peace is impossible: and it must be kindled soon, or war and revolution are at our gates.

For if mankind slumbers much longer in false security, in thoughtlessness, in a stupid indifference for justice, in a low selfishness, in carelessness of everything but robbery and gain, and in the filth of luxury and debauchery; then for fear they should stagnate to death, God will once more stir them up with revolution and war.

Be kindled then, O sacred Fire, and penetrate the nations, to lead them by the way of justice, faith, and knowledge, to unity, freedom, and peace.

O Jesus, who takest away the sins of the world, grant us Thy peace.

FINIS.

Published by Richardson and Son.

HYMNS FOR THE PEOPLE, adapted to popular tunes. Price 1d.

THANKSGIVING AFTER COMMUNION. From "ALL FOR JESUS." Price 1d. in wrapper.

A SCHEME OF INTERCESSORY PRAYER FOR THE MONTH. For the use of the Confraternity of the Precious Blood. Price 1d.

JESUS AND MARY, a Catholic Hymn Book. 1s.

THREE BEAUTIFUL PRINTS OF THE HOLY SOULS IN PURGATORY. With Verses. Price One Penny each.

THE LONDON ORATORY AND THE UNION NEWSPAPER. Being Three Letters on the Respect Due to Our Blessed Lord. 1d.

IN THE PRESS.

Second Edition (Fourth Thousand), with a copious Index, Price 6s.

SPIRITUAL CONFERENCES.

ALSO IN THE PRESS.

Third Edition (Sixth Thousand), with an INDEX. 6s.

GROWTH IN HOLINESS, or the Progress of the Spiritual Life.

Ready for the Press.

1. BETHLEHEM.
2. HYMNS AND SACRED POETRY.

Third Edition, cloth, 3s. 6d.

DEVOTION TO THE HEART OF JESUS, with an Introduction on the History of Jansenism. By the REV. FATHER DALGAIRNS, Priest of the Oratory.

THE NEW GLORIES OF THE CATHOLIC CHURCH, Translated from the Italian, by the Fathers of the London Oratory, at the request of the Cardinal Archbishop of Westminster, with a Preface by His Eminence, superfine paper, price 4s. 6d.

This work, which the Holy Father desires to have translated into all the languages of Europe, contains the Acts of the Recent Martyrs of the Corea, Cochin China, and Oceanica.

BOOKS FOR THE MONTH OF MAY.

Cloth lettered, price One Shilling.

THE CHILDREN'S BREAD; a Manual of Devotions for First Communicants. Followed by Devotions for Confirmation. Compiled by the Translator of "Hours at the Altar," and edited BY A FATHER OF THE BIRMINGHAM ORATORY.

Royal 32mo. cloth lettered, price 2s.

WALKING WITH GOD: or, DWELLERS IN THE RECREATION HOUSE OF THE LORD. Being a Translation from the Works of PERE RIGOLEUC, S.J. To which are added Two Meditations on the Hidden and Public Life of our Lord Jesus Christ, in which the principles set forth in the foregoing work are divinely and practically exemplified. Translated from the French by A RELIGIOUS of the Holy Child Jesus.

MONTH OF MAY; or Devout Exercises; comprising Meditations and Visits to the Sanctuaries of the Blessed Virgin, for every day in the month of May. To which are added, Prayers taken from the Saints and other Devout Writers, by the Rev. John Wyse. Cloth, red edges, 2s.

History of the Devotion to the Blessed Virgin Mary, Mother of God, Translated from the French of the Abbe Orsini, by the Rev. Patrick Power, with Episcopal Approbation, frontispiece, superfine cloth, lettered, 3s.

LILY OF ISRAEL; or the Life of the Blessed Virgin Mary, Mother of God. Translated from the French of the Abbe Gerbet. To which is added, the Veneration of the Blessed Virgin Mary. Superfine cloth, lettered, 3s.

CHILDREN OF MARY INSTRUCTED; or, a little book of Spiritual Reading and easy Prayers for young Children By a Mother. Demy 18mo., superfine cloth gilt, 2s.

VISITS TO THE SHRINES OF OUR LADY; Compiled from French and Italian authorities. By Edward G. Kirwan Browne. Handsome frontispiece, post 12mo, cloth gilt, 2s.

WREATH OUT OF THE ROSES OF LORETTO·
or Rhymes to our Lady, being a paraphrase of the Litany, written by a Convert, and edited by a Catholic Priest. Fine paper, demy 18mo., red border round each page, elegant engraved frontispiece, cloth, gilt edges, 1s.

PILGRIMAGE TO LA SALETTE;
by Bishop Ullathorne, 18mo. wrapper, 1s. 6d., superfine cloth, front, 2s.

Ursuline Month of May, by a Member of the
Ursuline Community, Blackrock, Cork. 18mo. cloth, 1s.

Devotion to the Holy Virgin ; or, the Knowledge
and Love of Mary, translated from the French of Father Gallifet, S.J., and dedicated to our Lady Help of Christians. Large type, cloth lettered, 6d.—embossed lettered. 8d.

CHILD'S MONTH OF MAY. New Edition, royal
32mo., printed cover, 2d.

Devout Prayers, in Honour of the Holy Name of
Mary, handsome wrapper, 2d.

Meditations as a Preparation for Whitsuntide and
other Feasts; together with such Methods and Helps in the practice of Mental Prayer and Examination of Conscience, as tend to the leading of a more Spiritual Life, royal 32mo, frontispiece, cloth, lettered, 6d.

Guide for Passing Holily the Time of Pentecost.
By Father Avrillon, Religious Minim, large royal 32mo., superfine paper, frontispiece, cloth lettered, 1s. 6d.

Prints with Prayers.

Acts of Dedication, or Triple Salutation of the
Blessed Virgin Mary, with engraving, 1d.

Month of May, or Pious Aspirations to the Mother
of God, for every day in the Month, by the Very Rev. Father Faber, D.D. With Print, 1d.

New Prayer to the Heart of Mary ; with a superior
engraving of the same, 1d.

Contract, or Prayer to be said once a week when
passing by our Lady's Altars and Pictures, with beautiful engraving, 1d.

☞ A great variety of Prints with Prayers and Hymns suitable for May, uniform with the above.

www.ingramcontent.com/pod-product-compliance
Lightning Source LLC
Chambersburg PA
CBHW031425020726
47499CB00005B/1603